GLORY'S LAST VICTIM

A Sharyn Howard Mystery

Other books by Joyce and Jim Lavene:

The *Sharyn Howard Mystery* Series

Last Dance
One Last Good-bye
The Last to Remember
Until Our Last Embrace
For the Last Time
Dreams Don't Last
Last Fires Burning

GLORY'S
LAST VICTIM

•

Joyce and Jim Lavene

AVALON BOOKS
NEW YORK

PRINTED IN THE UNITED STATES OF AMERICA
ON ACID-FREE PAPER
BY HADDON CRAFTSMEN, BLOOMSBURG, PENNSYLVANIA

For our friend, Daniel Bailey, who taught
us so much about real-life law enforcement.
And for Terry Hoover, president of the Tarheel Gumshoes'
chapter of Sisters-In-Crime: Thanks for all your hard work!

*"Mine eyes have seen the glory of the coming of the Lord,
He has trampled out the vintage where the grapes of
    wrath are stored,
He has loosed the fateful lightning of his terrible swift
    sword,
His truth is marching on."*

Prologue

She walked slowly through the moonlight, surrounded by the clean smell of the frozen earth. It was late. Too late to be out in the garden. But the night called to her and she answered. She'd been cooped up inside for too long. Stale air and too many people. Her breath misted into white ghosts as she laughed up at the clear bright stars.

She closed her eyes and drew the cold air into her warm lungs. Shivering in her thin nightgown, she knew she had to go back.

"What have we got here?" a coarse male voice asked.

Startled, she opened her eyes and started to run back to the house.

His hand snaked out and caught her arm. "Not leaving me alone already are you?"

"Let me go, please. My father will miss me. I have to go back inside."

"In a minute. First, let's have a little party."

Her heart thudded painfully in her chest. "It's late. I have to go."

The moonlight glinted on the knife in his hand. She knew she would never see her father again.

Chapter One

The woman was tall to begin with. Her bright red hair was swept artistically around her heavily made up face. She was perched precariously on six-inch heels. Her zebra-striped suit was garish in the neon lights from the mall. She was . . . noticeable.

The parking lot was almost empty near closing time. Ice crunched beneath her feet as she made a slow trip from the mall exit to her car. An oversized shopping bag filled one of her arms. An equally oversized purse slipped down her opposite shoulder to dangle from her fingers. She fumbled with her keys as she reached her car, finally dropping them on the pavement. She sighed and bent over to retrieve them, barely holding on to the huge purse.

Before she could stand upright, two young men flashed by her. One snatched her purse. The other grabbed her shopping bag. The boy, who grabbed her purse, cut the strap as he ran, taking a moment to push her backwards. It didn't take much. She was already unbalanced in the heels. With the shove, she sat down hard on the frozen concrete.

Immediately, a growl erupted from between the cars. An instant later, a fast moving form in a dark brown coat and pants jumped the first boy. They rolled in the icy parking lot together, finally coming to rest against the wheel of a car.

Another form stood up quickly in the parking lot, putting

herself in front of the second boy. "Uh-uh! Don't even think about it! You're busted!"

Ernie Watkins, head deputy sheriff for the small town of Diamond Springs and Montgomery County, North Carolina, offered his hand to the woman in the zebra-striped suit. "Cari got a mite excited."

Sheriff Sharyn Howard dusted snow and ice from her backside as she let Ernie help her to her feet. "I noticed. But it worked. We got the boys."

"Yeah." He laughed at her appearance. "With bait like that, how could we miss? I was almost tempted to take your pocketbook myself! You were a perfect victim!"

"Thanks. I think one of us should listen to Marvella doing Miranda."

"You do that. I don't want to strain myself before the wedding. I'll keep Cari from hurting that other boy."

"Do you think she's overcompensating for letting Chavis Whitley take her gun away and hold her hostage?"

"Just a tad. I'll talk to her again."

Sharyn went to listen to her newest deputy telling the purse-snatcher his rights. Marvella Honeycutt started out at the department as a janitor working her way through college. This was her first month on the job. She was a handsome black woman in her mid-30s with a knack for getting to the heart of any problem. Her attitude could be abrasive but Sharyn liked her and knew she'd be a good deputy.

"What's the matter with you, out here stealing a woman's purse?" Marvella was scolding the boy as she put handcuffs on him. "Where's your mama? I'm sure she'd be real proud of you doing this."

"I get a phone call," the boy told her.

"Phone call?" Marvella responded. "You'll be lucky if you ever see daylight again! Where's your brain anyway? You must've left it at home tonight!"

"Miranda?" Sharyn reminded her discreetly.

"Oh, yeah. You have the right to remain silent. Which I

think is a good idea 'cause no telling what fool thing is gonna come out of your mouth! You have the right to an attorney. And I suppose you'll be wanting the government to pay for it?"

Ernie shook his head as he joined Sharyn. "This is great. Cari is determined to be Wonder Woman and Marvella's trying to be Oprah. Maybe I should retire after all."

"You know, if you have a problem with something I'm doing," Marvella rushed in, "all you have to do is say so!"

"Let's get him in the car," Ernie answered. "Put him in with the other boy. I'll ride back to the office with the sheriff. You ride back with Cari."

"He doesn't like me," Marvella told Sharyn as she took her prisoner to the car. "What did I do to him?"

"He's cranky because of the wedding," Sharyn assured her. "It's nothing personal."

"Well, I hope he gets over it fast because I don't like the extra stress!"

Sharyn laughed and climbed into her Jeep. Brandy, the hairdresser/make-up expert at the Top Notch Salon de Beauty, went overboard with her hair and make-up. She looked more like a callgirl than a shopper. Fortunately, it drew the two boys out and that was all that mattered.

Those two boys had plagued the mall since Christmas, stealing from at least 25 shoppers. Extra sheriff's patrols didn't work. Neither did extra security guards. They picked their targets carefully then robbed them fast and efficiently. She was glad to finally move on to something else.

"That was clean and easy." Ernie climbed up into the Jeep beside her and shut the door on the cold night. "Although Cari's determined that there were more than two boys and thinks we should interrogate them."

Sharyn started the Jeep. Frost already covered the windows in the few hours they were there. It was a cold, hard winter. Lots of snow and ice. It was good after the dry, hot autumn but people had to remind themselves of that every frozen morning. "Do you think her problem is serious?"

"You mean does she need a shrink?" He grinned. "I don't think so. She's still a little messed up after that whole thing at the courthouse. She's determined to be tougher and more careful. I can't fault her there."

"I agree. To a point."

"I know. I know. I'll talk to her at the office. Reminds me a lot of another young woman who almost killed herself to prove how tough a sheriff she was!"

"Yeah, well, let's not let it get that far with Cari."

"Yes, ma'am."

"Now if we could catch that gang of burglars that easily."

"Yeah, but those guys are smart and they know their way around." Ernie looked at her in the passing lights from the Interstate. "You know, maybe you should keep that outfit. You could wear it to the wedding. It looks good on you."

"Yeah, right! Annie already told me what I'm supposed to wear *and* how unhappy she is that you've destroyed tradition by having a woman as your best man!"

"I knew she wouldn't like it. Believe me, she's been polite with you! I got an earful last night. Then her bridesmaids' dresses came in today and they were the wrong color. The flowers aren't what she wanted them to be and the caterer doesn't serve jasmine rice. Whatever that is!"

"Are you saying you should call the whole thing off?"

"Not on your life! I won't rest easy until we're married and she can't leave without me taking half her possessions." He played with his mustache. "That's the only way I know for sure she won't leave me flat. I *know* she loves that old house."

Sharyn laughed at him. "I think she loves you, too! Otherwise, she'd never put up with you. Late hours. Bad temper. Too bossy. Too nosy."

"That must be true. She could've dumped me a while back and not risked her house. What about you and Nick?"

"What about us?" She turned off the highway to Main Street.

"Have any thoughts about getting married?"

"Ernie, I thought you'd be happy we're dating! You were always ragging on me having someone in my life. Do we have to get married now?"

"I guess not. Not yet, anyway. Although if I was him, I wouldn't let you sit around too long. Old Jack Winter might sweep you up and carry you away!"

She shivered. "Don't even joke about that! Besides, he's at the Capitol now. We won't be seeing so much of him anymore. Good for us. Bad for those poor people."

"Hard to believe he took Talbot's senate seat away. I didn't think there was anyone who could do that. Speaking of which, how's Caison doing with your mama? Are the two of them thinking about getting married again?"

"Not yet." She smiled and waved to Charlie at the gate to the impound lot behind the sheriff's office. "At least not that I've heard. Who knows?"

"I didn't think they'd get back together. Faye had to swallow a lot of pride to take him back."

Sharyn turned off the engine. "You know, I think she really loves him. It was embarrassing for her to find out that he lied to her but I think she's going to get over it."

"What's he doing now?"

"Taking up his law career again. He's working on getting his son out of prison."

Ernie whistled between his teeth as he climbed down out of the Jeep. "That would be a mistake."

"I suppose if he were *your* son, you wouldn't think so."

"Evening, Sheriff," Charlie greeted her as he opened her car door. "I was almost ready to lock up for the night. Colder than Christmas out here."

Sharyn patted the retired deputy on the shoulder. "Go home and have a good night, Charlie. Have something nice and hot to drink!"

"I will, ma'am. After my shift at the museum. Paying off some Christmas bills by doing some part-time security work. Take care."

Ernie watched the other man get into his car. "You know, I hate to admit when I'm wrong."

"Really?"

"I was wrong about old Charlie. We needed more surveillance back here and better lighting. But you were right about not turning him out to pasture. He's good with those dogs too."

"I know." She smiled.

"Sass." He shook his head. "That's all I get from you."

"Yeah." She opened the door and a long, low wolf whistle accompanied her into the building.

"Is that the sheriff or a new international movie star?" Deputy Ed Robinson asked his partner, Joe Landers.

Joe removed his sunglasses, a rarity for him. "Can't be the sheriff. She ain't that *foxy!*"

"Must be a movie star!" Ed held out a paper for her to sign. "Can I get your autograph, ma'am?"

"What's this?" Ernie intercepted, glancing at the document. "Gun request? Who needs a new gun?"

"Marvella. We're taking her out to the range tomorrow," Ed told him.

"She hasn't had her six weeks' basic yet," Ernie reminded him. "We can't requisition a gun for her until she's here that long."

Marvella and Cari came in on the tail end of the conversation after dropping their prisoners off downstairs at the jail.

"Did I hear someone mention a gun?" Marvella asked, her dark eyes opening wide.

"You did," Ed replied. "But Ernie says not yet."

"You've only been working two weeks," Ernie reminded her, putting the gun request into the trash. "You have to go the whole six weeks."

"We thought she could help out with the Silver Dollar Gang," Joe added. "But we can't let her go out there unarmed."

"Not yet." Ernie was unmoved by their answers. "She's got another four weeks' basic training before she gets a gun."

They all looked at Sharyn even though it was her habit not to override Ernie on personnel issues. She didn't make an exception this time. "Sorry, boys. I have to go and slip into something less comfortable."

Marvella and Ed followed her into the locker room.

Sharyn glanced at them as she took her clothes out of her locker. "I meant *alone*."

"Sheriff, Ernie's being stubborn about Marvella. We could use the extra hand on this!"

"And I already know how to use a gun," Marvella persuaded. "I got one when I knew I was going to work as a deputy. I've been practicing ever since."

"That's not the same and this isn't something we can gloss over. Ernie's right. We're not that desperate. If you need help, let's call in a volunteer deputy."

"He doesn't like me, Sheriff," Marvella said again.

Ed slapped a locker. "I think he's being a stickler for the rules."

The locker room door opened again. The county medical examiner, Nick Thomopolis, and Ernie joined them.

Sharyn closed her locker door. "Maybe I should've changed out there so all of you could come in here!"

Ernie nudged Nick. "See? I told you. She looks pretty hot, doesn't she?"

"I don't know if *hot* is the word I'd use, but she looks different. Were you busting up a prostitution ring at the mall?"

Marvella *humphed* at Ernie and walked past him, leaving the locker room.

"What's wrong with her?" Nick asked.

"She's mad because Ernie won't let her have a gun," Ed answered.

"She's mad because you let her believe she *could* have a gun this early on," Ernie defended. "You were wrong to do that, Ed!"

"I thought we could bend the rules a little for once. I didn't know they were engraved in stone!"

Ernie watched Ed follow Marvella. "Guess I'll have to settle this. You two take your time and enjoy the sheriff's new look."

Nick waited until Ernie closed the door. "Who thought

about making you wear those heels? I'm surprised those boys weren't *afraid* to rob you!"

Sharyn tottered up next to him. With the heels, she was slightly taller than him. "I thought they'd be afraid of the outfit. I look like a really tall zebra."

Nick leaned close and kissed her. His dark eyes were intent on her face. "Do really tall zebras eat dinner?"

"This one does." She slid her fingers through his silvered black hair. "As soon as I change."

"I'm glad the election is over." He smiled at her. "We don't have to worry about upsetting Diamond Springs' protocol by telling everyone we're going out together. It never impressed anyone that I'm the county medical examiner. It's prestigious being known as the man who's dating the sheriff."

"Really?"

"Just today, my landlady asked me if I could get an extra patrol to come around since I'm the man who's dating the sheriff."

Sharyn laughed. "What did you say?"

"I offered to do it myself and showed her my gun collection and deputy's badge."

"I'll bet that impressed her! Not many people have two hundred guns. When do you start?"

"She turned me down. Told me I should stick to people who were already dead before I get myself in trouble."

"Sounds like good advice."

"Thanks. Maybe I should offer Marvella one of my guns!" Nick left her in the locker room and shut the door behind him.

Sharyn washed the make-up from her face and brushed the hairspray from her hair so it curled down against her shoulders again. She changed into jeans and a black sweater, taking a moment to admire her sleek, new look in the mirror.

She started working out at the gym before Christmas to keep from gaining the inevitable 10 pounds that collected. It worked, but she also liked the extra benefit of feeling toned and fit. It made up for those times when she sat behind her desk and ate junk food. Sometimes it was hard getting there.

She was thinking about asking the new county commission for a workout room at the sheriff's office.

The local election last fall brought some changes but mostly things stayed the same. All of the commissioners won their races. Except for Reed Harker who bowed out at the last minute. He decided that he didn't want to risk anything happening to his family because of decisions the commission made. His home was almost destroyed in November in retaliation for a commission ruling. He went back to working full-time as a real estate developer.

He was replaced by Julia Richmond, a young widow whose husband left her a fortune and lots of time to kill. Beau Richmond was highly regarded in the community until his death two years ago. His murder and the subsequent murder of her brother-in-law made a platform for Julia to run on. Everyone was concerned about the growing problem of crime in Diamond Springs. No one had any ready answers.

Of course, they all looked to the sheriff and her department to provide those answers. The voters felt good enough about what Sharyn was doing to re-elect her despite a heated campaign waged by an older, more experienced lawman. Even now, ex-sheriff Roy Tarnower was challenging her win in court. No one seemed to be overly concerned about it. Sharyn won by a sizeable number of votes.

She worried about the future of Diamond Springs like everyone else in town. Her father, T. Raymond, was the previous sheriff. His murder in a convenience store close to their home seemed to herald a new era of crime in town. Resources were strained for the sheriff's department to keep up with the county and the city. Shayrn hoped the new commission would be a little freer with funds to expand the sheriff's department.

The night shift was coming in as Sharyn was leaving with Nick. Ernie was already gone, pleading a major headache that was waiting for him at home. Trudy, their office manager, was arguing with Ed about going out for dinner. Since she'd agreed to date him once last year, he was on her like a bee on honeysuckle for a repeat performance.

"I only did it once to make you leave me alone," she told him as she got her things together.

Ed smiled at her. He was in his late 40s but he had a boyish face, curly blond hair and a way about him that got him plenty of female attention. "What are you afraid of, Trudy? It's only dinner. What's the big deal?"

"The big deal is *you*, Ed Robinson!" Trudy tossed her umbrella into her sizeable canvas purse. "I shouldn't have gone out with you at all! You don't know when enough is enough! Good night!"

Ed watched her leave. "I'll see you tomorrow, Sheriff."

"'Night, Ed."

He turned back to her. "You don't think I'm too pushy, do you?"

"If Trudy says no, it's no." Sharyn shrugged.

Ed's blue eyes were wounded. He turned to Nick. "I *know* you understand. If you took no for an answer, you wouldn't be dating right now."

Nick grinned. "Go for it. Whatever works this side of harassment."

Ed patted his shoulder. "Thanks, Nick."

"What did you just do?" Sharyn asked Nick as Ed ran out the door after Trudy.

"Played Cupid. Come on. Let's get out of here."

The two night shift deputies, David Matthews and JP Santiago, were checking out the reports coming in on the radio and by fax.

"'Night, boys," Sharyn said as she was leaving.

"Good night, Sheriff Howard," JP said with a broad grin. "Have a pleasant evening."

"Thanks."

"David still not talking to you?" Nick asked as they slipped out the back door.

"He's still broken hearted according to Ed."

"I've never known him to take so long getting over a woman," Nick remarked. "I might have to kill him for lusting after you."

"I don't think I'd call it that. Where are we going for dinner?"

"Fuigi's. Unless you think they might recognize you from your time at the mall tonight and refuse to let us in."

"Ha-ha." She followed him into the parking lot. "Your car or mine?"

"Mine. We have a better chance of making it there without someone calling you. There's something about your Jeep."

"It's a crime magnet?"

"I think that's it."

Nick drove his new black Cadillac SUV down Main Street towards the Interstate then veered off suddenly towards Diamond Lake. "I forgot something. Do you mind running to my apartment?"

"No. That's okay. I thought you kept your guns in the trunk?"

He grinned. "Not all of them."

"Nick—"

"Relax! You don't have to bust me for illegal possession of firearms. And I'm not going back for a gun. I wanted to set up to tape Star Trek tonight."

"You're putting me off for Star Trek? Knowing someone could call and ruin dinner at any moment?"

"Some things are more important than food."

She followed him up to his apartment, deciding not to wait in the parking lot. His landlady nodded to them as they walked by her door but she retreated quickly.

"It'll only take a minute," he convinced Sharyn as he opened the door.

"I think you shook your landlady's faith in the sheriff's department. She probably won't call even if someone takes everything she has."

"It was bound to happen." He let her walk in before him. "Everyone gets disillusioned with real-life crime. It's not as interesting as the stuff on TV."

The apartment was dark as she walked in, then all of the lights came on at once.

"Surprise! Happy birthday!"

Sharyn blinked her eyes and saw Ernie and Annie, Trudy and Ed, Joe and his wife, Sarah. Her mother was there with her sister, Kristie, and her Aunt Selma. "You tricked me," she accused Nick.

He took her jacket and kissed her. "All the better to surprise you, my dear sheriff. Happy birthday."

"But it's not for three days," she protested.

"It looked like tonight was going to be quiet." Ernie hugged her for a moment. "We didn't want to take any chances."

"Besides," Kristie assured her, "we needed a party. And I start school next week."

"I'm not complaining," Sharyn hugged her. "I hope we're eating whatever that is that smells so good!"

"Nick made lasagna," Sharyn's mother told her. "Kristie and I brought the salad and bread."

"And I made the dessert," Annie said, hugging her. "Your favorite, I think. Red velvet cake."

Sharyn patted her stomach. "And I thought I wasn't going to gain any weight from the holidays."

They all sat down at the big table in Nick's dining room. He served the lasagna, starting with Sharyn, who sat at the head of the table with a birthday princess crown on her head.

"I have some big news," Kristie confided from Sharyn's right side.

"What's that?"

"I took a job working on Jack Winter's staff."

Sharyn's attention riveted on her younger sister. Her bright golden hair was growing out from being shaved and dyed purple. The pin that was in her nose was gone. The scars on her neck left by an attack on her last year would never be gone. But she was recovering emotionally. "What do you mean?"

"I mean, I'm going back to school and I'm going to be close to Jack Winter's office in Raleigh. I volunteered to help out. I thought I could keep an eye on him for you that way."

"Kristie, you can't get involved with him. He's dangerous."

"Sharyn, I want to help. Let me do this!"

Ignoring the two sisters whispering together, the conversation at the table grew louder and finally reached them.

"Birthday speech!" Ed called out. "Let's hear what the newly elected sheriff has to say on her big three–oh!"

Everyone turned to face her. Sharyn knew she couldn't talk to Kristie any more about it then. But she wouldn't let it drop either. The idea of her being in close proximity to former DA Jack Winter made her shudder.

Winter was unscrupulous. He'd do anything to get what he wanted, including ruining his best friend and former associate, Caison Talbot, for his senate seat. A dark question still lurked in the shadows about Winter being involved in her father's death.

Sharyn was convinced that he had their house firebombed in November to make sure whatever he was looking for in her father's papers was never found. In some ways, she admitted that it might be a blessing. She didn't want to find out that her father was in league with the DA during his time as sheriff. But if that's what it took to put Winter away, she was more than willing to face it.

Sharyn got to her feet giving Kristie a look that told her they'd talk about it later. "I'd like to thank all of you for being here tonight and for supporting me through the election. You've all made my job a lot easier and I wouldn't want to be sheriff without you."

"It wasn't always that way, was it, Sharyn?" Aunt Selma spoke up.

"No," Sharyn admitted. "But it worked out."

"No." Joe got to his feet. "She's right. We gave you a hard time when you first came in and took T. Raymond's place. None of us were sure you could do the job. Most of us thought you were too young and too inexperienced."

"Except for Ernie." Ed gave the head deputy his due. "He always believed in you."

Ernie grinned and looked wise as his fiancée squeezed him tight and smiled at him.

"So, now's a good time for us to admit we were wrong," Joe said. "You're a good sheriff. And a good friend."

"Here, here!" Ed agreed.

They all looked at Nick as he took a seat at the other end of the long table. He looked back at them. "What?"

"Isn't there something you want to say, Mr. Medical Examiner?" Joe demanded, sitting down.

"Yeah, I think *you* doubted how she'd do more than any of us," Ed added with a laugh.

"I seem to recall that you even gave in your resignation at one point," Ernie helped out, with a smile at Sharyn.

"That's true," Nick agreed, pyramiding his hands together as he looked at Sharyn across the table. "And I was wrong. I admit it. My only excuse is that she was driving me crazy. Even then. Eventually, I realized that I couldn't fight it."

"That would be the night of the high school reunion." Ernie chuckled. "When I saw you dance with her, I knew the two of you were gonna be good together."

Nick raised his wine glass to her. "Happy birthday, Sharyn. I wish you many more."

They all agreed. Then the doorbell rang. It was Cari and her date, ADA Toby Fisher. Marvella and her husband, Harvey, were there too. They squeezed in at the table. The conversation went from loud to boisterous. Nick's landlady thumped on the wall and they laughed but kept their voices down.

Annie served cake while Nick made coffee. Sharyn tried to get her sister alone in the room but she was the center of attention. It was impossible to end one conversation without starting another.

"I heard something about the new commission taking up the idea of separating Diamond Springs and the county. Creating a police department for the town and moving the sheriff's department out into the county," Toby Fisher said as they all sat together.

"That's crazy!" Joe announced.

"Not really. The sheriff's department would still have jurisdiction in town on the felonies, but the police department would handle the small stuff that weighs you all down now."

"You heard that, Sheriff?" Ed asked her.

"No. I didn't hear that one yet," Sharyn admitted. "But it's a new commission. They could do anything."

"If they gave us the money that would cost, it would take care of the problem," Joe told Toby.

Toby shrugged and glanced at Cari. "It's what I heard today."

Cari smiled at him and gave him a cup of coffee.

"It makes sense," Sharyn continued unexpectedly. "Most counties do have a sheriff's department for the county and a police department for the bigger towns."

"I'm not chasing or catching cows, foxes, ferrets or any other animals if they do that," Joe promised. "If they have the money to create a whole new police department, they better bring back animal control!"

Nick sat down beside Sharyn on the wide brown sofa. "I wonder if that would mean you'd work from the county jail instead of Diamond Springs?"

"Not necessarily. In Cabarrus County, the sheriff's office is in Concord. Maybe they'll give us a new office with a workout room."

"That's all you think about!" her mother protested. "Since we moved into the apartment while the house is being repaired, she works out non-stop. I hardly ever see her!"

No one remarked on it. Everyone knew that Faye and Sharyn's relationship could be strained at times. Putting them together in a two-bedroom apartment might make things worse if one of them wasn't gone a lot.

"How are things going with Caison?" Nick asked, changing the subject.

Faye blushed attractively. "I think something very good is going to come out of that whole sordid mess. I don't know what it will mean for the future. But I think we've both changed."

Sharyn sipped her coffee. Her mother was holding her secrets close. Maybe she was afraid to be so forthcoming again. After announcing their engagement before backing out of it, she was bound to be nervous. Who knew what other skeletons were lurking in Talbot's closet?

The party was breaking up and everyone was leaving. They thanked Nick for a great time as they walked out the door. Sharyn grabbed her sister as Kristie was going to leave, offering to take her home if her aunt was in a hurry.

"I'll wait." Selma took a seat in the kitchen. "I'd like a little more coffee if you've got it, Nick. What do you put in that?"

"A touch of cinnamon," he told her, getting the pot.

Kristie sat beside Sharyn on the sofa. "What's up?"

"I don't want you trying to spy on Jack Winter."

"Why? I want to help you! I've heard you talking about him trying to find papers that belonged to Dad. The man's no good. All of you say so. Why shouldn't I help you with him? He won't suspect me."

Sharyn shook her head. "He suspects everyone. He doesn't trust anyone, Kristie. He won't trust you. He'll be waiting for you to make a mistake and then he'll pounce."

"I'm not a helpless mouse, Sharyn. I know what I'm doing. You may be braver than me but you're not smarter or more determined."

"Kristie—"

Sharyn struggled for words that would keep her sister away from the ex-DA of Diamond Springs.

Her pager went off a second before she heard Ernie's pager. He glanced up at her. "You too? It must be something big."

Chapter Two

The young couple looked like owls standing together in the doorway of the pricey new home.

"We just got back from England," the man said as Sharyn approached him. "We were on our honeymoon. We've barely moved in and this happened to us!"

"I'm sorry, Mr . . . ?"

"Blair Stuckey." He stuck out his hand. "This is my wife, Marcia. We moved here last month from Charlotte. We thought this area was quiet, a good place to raise kids."

"We never had a break-in when we lived in Charlotte," Marcia said quietly.

"It usually *is* quiet," Sharyn told them. "We've got a group of people who are robbing the new houses in this area. I'm sorry you had to come home to this."

"Did you have an alarm system?" Ernie asked when he joined them.

"We waited to activate it until we came back," Marcia explained. "We thought it was a joke that we had it at all."

Ernie was already looking at the door. "It's the same. They picked the lock."

"I've got a call in to our forensics people," Sharyn told Marcia and Blair. "They'll be out to take a look around and see what they can find that will help us catch the people who did this."

"We'll need you to go through and make a list of everything

18

that's missing," Ernie added. "Deputy Long will walk through with you. Try not to touch anything until forensics gets a look at it."

Marcia and Blair nodded miserably.

"Right!" Cari nodded stiffly. "Let's go!"

"It looks like the Silver Dollar Gang." Joe came around the side of the house. "Big house with plenty of money, jewelry, and electronic stuff. There's a whole media wall that's empty."

"There's a full moon," Ernie remarked after he got Cari and the couple started on their walk through the house. "They seem to like that."

"No wonder," Ed answered. "It's dark out here."

"Streetlights are up but not on," Marvella remarked pointing at them.

"The neighborhood is too new. That's one of the reasons they're picking on it," Sharyn said.

Ed came up next to her. "If you don't mind, Sheriff, I'm gonna take Trudy home while it's not too late to go in for some coffee."

"That's fine," Sharyn told him. "I think we're a little over-staffed here anyway. Thanks for the birthday party. It was nice."

He reached over and hugged her tightly. "'Night, Sheriff."

Sharyn pulled down her sweater, amazed by his unusual emotional display.

"What?" Ed looked around at the other surprised faces. "We aren't really on duty and we aren't in uniform. I've known her since she was knee high to a grasshopper."

Ernie looked skeptical.

"And Trudy says I'm not sensitive enough. I'm working on it."

Joe shook his head. "Good night all."

Sharyn groaned and moved away from Ed. "Would you like me to start calling you Uncle Ed?"

"Do you think Trudy would like it?"

"I'm going home too," Ernie announced. "Nick's here."

"David's out on patrol and JP is settling a domestic dispute.

That's why our pagers went off," Sharyn explained. "I'll keep everyone posted."

Cari was still walking through the house with the Stuckeys. Sharyn could hear them crying and exclaiming as they discovered their losses. She had to think of some way to put an end to the break-ins.

She saw Nick walk up to the house. The black van that carried his forensics team was right behind him. "Another one?"

"Looks like it."

He pulled on his gloves. "You know, this area is going to get a bad rep before it's even finished."

"I know. There has to be some way to stop them."

"You might as well go too. Not that I wouldn't like to have you tag along while we go through all of this but I don't have to be up working in the morning and you do."

She didn't argue with him. "Let me know what you find out."

"Report on your desk first thing in the morning. Go home. Get some sleep." He kissed her quickly before the van door opened and his team piled out.

"Wow! Somebody got another one of these elephants!" Megan said with a shake of her bright pink hair. She was one of Nick's assistants from the local college.

"Good luck, Nick." Sharyn left him. "Thanks for the party. Hello, Megan."

"Hi Sheriff. This place makes me gag, you know? We're way too capitalistic in this country!"

"Maybe you're right."

Keith Reynolds and several of Nick's pathology students pushed their way into the house.

"Do we get extra credit for this, Professor?" one boy asked, seeing the mess.

"You're getting extra credit for being here," Nick reminded him. "Everyone get your gloves on!"

Sharyn knew they were lucky to have Nick as county medical examiner since the county budget wouldn't stretch to assistants. He used his students from his forensics class at the college to get the work done. They got extra credit and Diamond Springs didn't have to rely on state assistants who only came through on an irregular basis. She knew he planned to ask for more money from the new commission too. She hoped there was enough to go around for everyone from the larger tax base.

Sharyn drove back into the heart of Diamond Springs. She parked her Jeep on the street since the apartment she was sharing with her mother didn't have a garage. The insurance company leased the apartment for them while the repairs were being done. The contractor said it wouldn't be more than a few months.

She shivered as she locked her car and headed for the door to their apartment. It felt like it was getting colder. The wind was always stronger close to the lake so it was hard to tell.

The light was on upstairs but there was no sign of Caison's limo. The ex-senator still had plenty of money. She supposed his personal family fortune would carry him through the rest of his life. She was surprised that he wasn't at the birthday party with her mother. Even though her mother was seeing him again, Sharyn didn't see much of him. Everything he went through left him a changed man. More vulnerable. Less domineering. But she still avoided him whenever possible. There was something distinctly underhanded about him.

"Sharyn?"

She turned sharply and found herself face-to-face with Jack Winter. The newly elected senator stepped into the pale light from the street. He was 30 years older than Sharyn but his features were strong, clearly defined. A high forehead sloped down to pallid blue eyes that were sharper than razors. If a man's soul could be read in his eyes, she felt sure his would scream evil, beware!

"Senator Winter," she greeted him coolly although her heart was pounding. *What was he doing here?* "What brings you back to Diamond Springs so soon? I thought they'd have plenty to keep you busy at the Capitol."

"I expected to be invited to your birthday party." His lips stretched into a thin smile. "Then your mother told me that she decided against including me. Something about her new found relationship with Caison."

She nodded. "They're back together now."

"You know I'm happy for them."

"Really? I thought you wanted to have that relationship with my mother."

"Not really." His gaze raked her. "I've always fancied redheads."

She nearly choked on the implication behind his words.

"Don't bother telling me how much you're repelled by me, Sharyn. I only stopped by to tell you happy birthday. And congratulations on the election. You did it."

"Thanks," she ground out from between clenched teeth.

"Good luck. I'll be seeing you around."

Not if I see you first!

"Oh. I hired your sister the other day. She wanted to work with my staff in Raleigh. I'm looking forward to getting to know her better. She's not like you, of course. But she's very lovely."

"She won't be working for you. That was a mistake."

He laughed. "We'll see. I could persuade her to go and work someplace else, if you like."

"I think I can do that without your help."

"Suit yourself. I'd be happy to take you in place of her." He stepped closer and reached out a hand to touch her face. "My offer still stands even though I'm not DA here anymore. I would love to have you with me."

Sharyn's service revolver was wedged between them before his finger drew a line down her cheek.

"You've become very jumpy, Sharyn. You need to calm down. Take a vacation." He lowered his hand like he didn't know the gun was there against his heart. "I'd hate for an accident to happen. Something you might regret forever, hmm?"

"Go away, Jack. Leave me alone."

"Good night, Sharyn. Sweet dreams."

She watched him walk away down the street until he reached his waiting car near the corner. Her breath came out frosty in the cold night air. Her hands were frozen on her gun. She made herself put it back in the holster. He was right. She had to stop reacting to him. The man lived for it. She walked upstairs to her apartment and double locked the door behind her.

"Sharyn, you should see this." Her mother woke her the next morning.

"What is it?" Sharyn's face was muffled against her pillow. She finally fell asleep an hour before dawn. Jack Winter haunted her nightmares.

"Another girl was attacked at Piper College."

"*Another* girl?" she asked, finally catching her mother's words.

"Yes. Don't you remember? A girl was killed there four or five years ago. Another one was attacked last night."

"Was she killed?"

"They aren't saying. But they've arrested a suspect."

"Who is it?" Sharyn joined her mother at the tiny TV in the kitchen.

"Police in the small town of Rock Springs have told us that they have arrested a suspect in the attack on twenty-two-year-old Lynette Ashe last night. He is fifty-year-old Samuel Two Rivers of Montgomery County, North Carolina."

"Oh my!" Faye put her hand to her lips. "Your Aunt Selma's new beau!"

Sharyn wasn't sure if she was more amazed by what she heard from the reporter on TV or what her mother was saying. "*What?*"

"Hey! Did you hear about them arresting Sam last night?"

Sharyn took off her jacket at the door to the sheriff's office. "Yeah."

"I don't believe he attacked that girl." Ernie handed her a

cup of coffee. "He doesn't fit the profile of someone who'd do something like that."

"Me either. I heard something even stranger. It seems that he and Aunt Selma have been seeing each other."

Ernie's lips twitched. "That must account for why she's here in your office already this morning."

Sharyn frowned. "She must know there's not much I can do. It's in another county."

"She's *your* aunt. I wouldn't want to tell her anything like that. She might hurt me."

"Did you get the list of missing items from the Stuckeys' last night?"

"Yeah. Cari was out there until midnight with them. She brought it in this morning."

"The usual?"

"Yeah. Computer components. Stereo. Jewelry. Cash. Coin collection. Antique vase."

"Thanks."

"Did you see the paper yet this morning?" He held it up for her.

"They gave them a name?"

"Last week. Where've you been? The Silver Dollar Gang. Catchy, huh?"

"Yeah. Like a bad cold."

"I'll start adding the info to the spreadsheet. I think you better talk to your aunt."

She opened the door to her office. "Morning, Aunt Selma."

"Good morning, Sharyn." Her aunt stood up and hugged her. "How are you and Faye doing in the apartment?"

"Good. As long as one of us is always out."

"Of course!"

Sharyn slung her backpack down on her old wooden desk. Her grandfather and father looked down at her from their place on the wall. Her grandfather, Jacob, was the first sheriff elected in Diamond Springs. She followed in his footsteps by being the first woman elected as sheriff in the state of North

Carolina. They were all reflected in her father's sister's face. "I heard about Sam."

Selma nodded. She was the matriarch of the Howard clan, keeping the memories and the homestead alive for the family. Her red hair was growing white in places, spilling down her neck from the bun on her head. She was a handsome woman whose youthfulness belied her true age. Her blue eyes burned into her niece's. "You know Sam didn't attack that girl."

Sharyn took her seat across the desk from her aunt. "I don't know him very well but I like him. He doesn't seem capable of this kind of act."

"He isn't. He was only at Piper College because I was there. You know I teach that course every year on herbs and such. If he weren't visiting me there, he wouldn't be involved at all. I don't know exactly what happened but I know he didn't hurt that girl."

"I'm sure the police will get to the bottom of it. Mom said there was a murder there a few years back."

"A murder they never solved! I need your help, Sharyn. I'm sure they have him tried and convicted already. You could find the real criminal."

"Aunt Selma, that's a different county. There isn't anything I can do unless they ask for my help."

"You can find out why they arrested him and what happened. They won't talk to me. They're keeping the details quiet for some reason. They won't let me see him. *You* could see him. He could tell you why they arrested him."

"I've got five local robberies unsolved on my desk. Last night, another one happened in the same area. I'd like to help but I don't have time to visit the police in Rock Springs and find out why they arrested Sam."

Selma Howard's jaw was tight. "I never ask you for any favors!"

Sharyn laughed. "Not unless you need something!"

The older woman got to her feet. "I didn't know you felt that way. I'll find another way to learn what happened. I'm sorry I bothered you."

Sharyn pushed her hair back from her face. She couldn't let her leave that way. "All right. I'm sorry. I'll call Rock Springs and see what they'll tell me. That's the best I can do. Okay?"

"Thank you. Shall I call you or will you call me?"

"I'll call you when I know something."

"I appreciate it. Sam means a lot to me. And I know he isn't guilty of this crime. He's a very gentle man. And he's not the type to be interested in a young girl, like they were saying on campus this morning."

"I didn't know you were seeing him." Sharyn smiled at her. "How long have you two been together?"

"You didn't need to know. We were friends for a while. He came out to take a look at my bees. It became something more." Selma laughed at herself. "I suppose you think I'm a silly, bossy old woman."

"Bossy?" Sharyn laughed with her. "Yes! Silly? Never. But it wouldn't hurt if you were sometimes. I've never even known you to date."

"There's probably a few things I've managed to keep secret." Selma hugged her again. "I'll talk to you later. Call me when you know anything."

Sharyn sat back down at her desk and shook her head.

"She wants you to check up on him, doesn't she?" Ernie joined her when he saw her aunt leave the office.

"I know you're not surprised."

"And you said no," he persisted. "Then you agreed to do it?"

"Ernie, it's too early for mind reading."

"Okay. Well, then how about the night shift report and what we found out at the Stuckeys' house last night?"

"That's fine. Thanks."

"The domestic disturbance JP handled last night turned ugly. He arrested the man and *both* women."

She raised her cinnamon-colored eyebrows. "Sounds like fun."

"David answered a call about bats in a woman's house and

helped out with an accident caused by a man at the Wendy's around two A.M. Turns out that the man in the car ordering french fries was naked and couldn't get out when he dropped them on the ground. He demanded that the man in the window come out and get them for him. When he didn't, the naked man decided to ram his car into the drive through."

"Was anyone hurt?"

"No. JP and David arrested the man in the car."

"And you thought the night was going to be quiet!"

"Nick sent this report over when he was finished looking through the house last night." He pushed the paper on her desk. "He agrees that it was the Silver Dollar Gang. But they were able to collect one thumbprint."

"Any takers?"

"Not yet. He's got his computer scanning data bases."

She looked up from the paper. "Why isn't he—"

"He's got a meeting with the commissioners this morning. Trying to wheedle more money out of them. I expect you'll be over there soon enough."

"Good luck." Sharyn filed the report. "So we might actually have something to go on with the break-ins."

"Looks like." He got up from his chair and picked up his coffee cup. "I guess you'll need to make that call to the police department in Rock Springs now, huh? Selma and Sam Two Rivers. Who'd guess?"

"She said they met when he came to look at her bees."

"I told the commission they should ban beekeeping if they wanted to uphold the strict moral code in this county!"

She laughed. "Go away, Ernie! I have a phone call to make."

"And some clout to wield?" He chuckled and left her alone.

The police chief in Rock Springs, Howell Murray, was helpful and courteous. "I don't know what I can tell you, Sheriff Howard. We found Mr. Two Rivers crouched down beside the girl on the grounds of the college. He was covered in her blood and holding the knife. He was a little wild when we tried to bring him in. He's a big man. My deputy was afraid for his life. We had to get stern with him."

Sharyn translated that. "Was he hurt during the arrest?"

"A little banged up. We tried not to hurt him. He's okay. Except that he won't say a word. Didn't want his phone call. We're taking him over to the mental hospital today. They think he might be catatonic. Maybe too horrified to speak or think after what he did to that poor girl."

"How's the girl?"

"She's hanging in there. The doctor says it will take time to see if she survives. It wasn't a pretty sight. She was really messed up."

Sharyn was doodling on a piece of paper on her desk. "I'd like to see him, if you don't mind."

"Mr. Two Rivers?"

"Yes. If it's possible. I might be able to persuade him to talk to me. I've known him for a while. He's worked with the sheriff's department here a few times."

"I don't see what good it would do. We don't really need his confession."

"Well, if he talks to me, I could spare you the expense and time of taking him to Morganton. No guarantee, but it could work seeing someone he knows."

The police chief agreed reluctantly. "I guess you could take a pass at him, Sheriff. So long as you don't expect too much. We'll hold off until you can talk to him."

"Thanks, Chief Murray. I'll be there as soon as I can."

Ernie caught her as she was leaving the office. "Going to Rock Springs?"

"Yeah. Keep me posted if anything shows up here. I thought I'd take Marvella with me to keep her out of trouble."

"Too late. Ed and Joe have taken their 'adopted daughter' with them on patrol."

"That's probably good."

"It would be," he agreed, "except that I'm going to have to catch them out down at the shooting range in about ten minutes."

"I don't even want to know how you found out."

"I can't believe those two are being such idiots about this! I thought they didn't like Marvella?"

"They do now. I'll be back as soon as I can."

"Don't answer your phone! They'll probably be whining to you about it!"

Sharyn went outside. She didn't like the idea of getting involved in another county's processes. Especially for a family member. But none of this sounded like Sam. He could be a little sharp and sarcastic but it was hard to believe that he could hurt anyone.

Unless the girl was attacking an animal on Diamond Mountain. He and Bruce Bellows, the local wildlife administrator, were passionate about conserving the wild animals that lived there. Maybe he was at the wrong place at the wrong time. He might have stumbled across the attack. Maybe even tried to help. She didn't know what to think about him not speaking to the police.

Charlie waved to her from the gate. The dogs barked in their kennel. They were only released at night after everyone went home. They kept the impound lot free of anyone who didn't belong there. Sharyn unlocked her Jeep and started to climb in when she saw it.

A gold and lace wrapped gift sat squarely on the black driver's seat. A small card was attached. She looked quickly around her but there was no one else in the back lot. With Charlie at the gate, the only other way in was to walk back from the courthouse. The area was restricted but a person with a pass card could do it. Of course, *he* could do it.

Not that it accounted for how the gift came to be there in her *locked* vehicle. But she knew who it was from before she read the card. *"A token of my sentiments. Jack."*

"Hey, are you getting in or standing there with your mouth open?"

She quickly hid the small package behind the seat. "A little of both. What are *you* doing?"

"Going with you," Ernie announced cheerfully. "Cari is logging that information into the computer. I decided you could go with me to the shooting range to add an extra foot to my kicking certain deputy's butts. Then I could go with you to Rock Springs."

She got behind the wheel. Her mind was still working over the gift left in her Jeep. "I guess that will work."

He climbed up into the passenger's seat and looked at her. "What's wrong, Sheriff?"

She started the engine. "Nothing. Just thinking about Sam and the break-ins."

Ernie frowned. "I think I've remarked before on what a poor liar you are. You look like you've seen a ghost."

"It's nothing."

He fastened his seatbelt. "Okay. You don't want to talk about it. I know when to back off."

She laughed. "Sure you do."

They drove in silence towards the shooting range that was at the outskirts of town. It actually belonged to a gun club that let the sheriff's department use it for practice.

"What are you going to do when we get there?" she asked him.

"I don't know yet."

"That's comforting. I didn't know you were such a seat-of-your-pants kind of guy."

"This isn't easy. Joe and Ed have been my friends for a long time. I don't know what's wrong with them. I think Marvella put a hex on them to scramble their brains."

Sharyn pulled the Jeep into the crude parking area marked by ropes across the gravel drive. There was a rough shelter where they sold ammunition or a cold Coke. She could see Ed and Joe standing beside Marvella on the frosty hill. Marvella was firing a gun at a target.

"Well, I've decided," Ernie told Sharyn. "I'm going to bite their heads off."

She turned off the engine and got out after him. "And what did you want me to do?"

"Look supportive and don't say anything. If I can't handle this, I'm no good to you."

They ducked under the rope barrier and walked out to the range. The man in the shelter saluted them as he drank a cup of coffee. It steamed up into the cold air and spread the pungent aroma to them. Sharyn got an idea who'd tipped Ernie.

Ed saw them coming before they reached them. He shook his head and spoke to Joe and Marvella. Marvella handed the gun to Joe and turned to face them.

Ernie stopped and looked at them. "I know you two aren't out here teaching her to shoot after I said she couldn't use a gun yet!"

"Aww, Ernie, you're bent out over nothing," Ed started. "It's not gonna hurt anything."

"Is that it? Because I thought I was in charge of personnel. I thought we were running a professional sheriff's department. You both know the department isn't carrying insurance on Marvella using a gun until she's finished training. What part about that don't you get?"

"It's my fault, Ernie." Marvella stepped forward. "I had them bring me out here."

"You're right," he agreed. "And you're confined to desk duty the rest of this week. You'll have to take an extra week for training in the field."

"Ernie!" Joe began angrily. "We need another hand!"

"Then I suggest you find someone qualified to be that hand, Deputy! This woman isn't. Get your stuff together and get her back to the office! You don't have to remind me that we're short on help. If we weren't, I'd tie the two of you to desks for the week too!"

Joe stalked back towards the patrol car without another word.

Ed shook his head and ran his hand through his curls. "Ernie, you can be a real pain sometimes." He glanced at Sharyn. "Sheriff."

She nodded at him and swallowed hard. She was glad she wasn't on the other end of Ernie's tongue-lashing.

"I'm sorry, Ernie." Marvella was contrite. "I didn't mean to get anyone in trouble. I thought I could speed up the process."

"You can't do that. Now go on back to the office."

Marvella looked at Sharyn but didn't speak to her.

Sharyn took a deep breath of the cold air and wrapped her arms across her chest. "Okay. That was exciting. Can we go to Rock Springs now?"

Ernie nodded and stomped back towards the Jeep. He jerked open the door and slammed it shut. Sharyn opened her door and the gift she was hiding rolled out to the ground at her feet.

"What's that?"

She looked at him and smiled awkwardly. "Nothing."

"Looks like a birthday present."

"It is, I guess." She heard the gold paper tear as she stuffed it under the seat and climbed behind the wheel.

"You're not going to open it?"

"It's not my birthday yet." She started the engine and pulled back out on the highway.

"Who's it from?"

"Nobody. It doesn't matter." She turned the Jeep towards Rock Springs.

Ernie shifted uneasily in his seat. "I'd say you didn't want Nick to be jealous but then you wouldn't mind telling me 'cause you know I wouldn't tell him."

"Ernie, could you drop it? You're like a dog with a bone sometimes. It's a birthday gift. I'm not going to open it."

"Whatever you say, Sheriff."

"Thanks."

"So, what are you gonna say to old Howell Murray about him holding Sam?"

Glad to be back on familiar ground, Sharyn relaxed. "I'm going to find out about the case against him. Maybe talk to him and see what happened. The chief said he hasn't said a word and he doesn't want to make a phone call. He hasn't asked for a lawyer."

"Have they actually arrested him because they have evidence against him? Or are they holding him because they're looking at him for it?"

"I'm not sure. Murray said they found him next to the girl on the Piper campus. He was holding a knife and covered in her blood. He acted wild and wouldn't talk to them. I would've picked him up too."

"What did Selma say?"

"She said he was there visiting her at the college. She's teaching a class down there on herbs and naturopathic healing. She's done it for a couple of years now."

"Sounds bad." Ernie glanced at the rock that was encrypted with the sign for the town. ROCK SPRINGS POPULATION 2,000. A NICE PLACE TO LIVE.

"I know."

There wasn't much in Rock Springs besides Piper College. It sprawled across 20 acres in the middle of town. The original building was an old plantation house that had been renovated several times down through the years. It was used as the main office. The rest of the gray stone buildings were added as time passed. Despite losing some federal funding, the school remained an elite women's college since it began in 1865. Women came from all over the world to attend classes.

The police station and the post office were in the same gray stone building across the street from the main office of the college. There was a diner and a beauty salon next to them. That was what made up downtown Rock Springs. There was talk of building a Hardee's but nothing came of it yet. Traffic was light since the Interstate was 20 miles away. Piper maintained its air of timeless serenity.

Sharyn and Ernie were told that Chief Murray was out for a while but the deputy showed them back to Sam's cell. The steel-barred door locked behind them.

Sam Two Rivers looked up at them. His face was swollen, badly beaten. His long, iron gray hair was loose around his shoulders. He opened his mouth. *"S-gi-na."*

Chapter Three

"I can't help you if you don't tell me what happened," Sharyn told Sam for the third time. "We're all concerned about you. Why won't you let us help?"

Sam's rugged face was expressionless. His black eyes stared into the distance with no sign that he heard or recognized her.

She took a deep breath and sat back on the small bed beside him in the cell. "I don't know what to say. Maybe Chief Howell is right. Maybe he needs help."

Ernie leaned against the wall. "I understand a little Cherokee. He said *s-gi-na* when we first walked in. I'm not sure what that means, what he was trying to tell us."

The door opened to the area that held the two cells. "Sheriff Howard? I'm Chief Howell Murray. We don't take to much formality around here so please call me Howell."

"Thanks, Howell." She got to her feet as he was opening the cell door. "I'm Sharyn."

"Were you able to get anything out of him, Sharyn?"

"No," she answered with a glance at Ernie. "He hasn't said anything."

"I'm head deputy Ernie Watkins. I think we met a few years back at a conference in Raleigh."

Howell Murray was broad faced with a thick head of curly brown hair. In his youth, he was a ladies' man. Some of that still lingered in his gaze. His handshake was strong, his manner was open and positive. "I seem to recall that, Deputy. I think that was back before your old sheriff was killed."

"I think so. Sharyn is his daughter."

"Well, I'll be! You know, I remember reading about that during the last election! Congratulations on that win, Sharyn! I'm glad I don't have to go through that kind of thing here. Of course, some days I think it might be a blessing to have someone elect me out of here!"

They walked back through the cell door. The officer closed the door behind them. Howell introduced them to Pike Kaiser, his only employee and son-in-law.

"I heard about there being a lady sheriff in Montgomery County." Pike took her hand and smiled. "Nice to meet you."

"Thanks." Sharyn sat down between the two desks in the single cramped office. It reminded her that she should be glad she had as much space as she did at her office. Even without the work-out room. "So, what can you tell me about the attack?"

"Well, like I told you, the girl is still alive. The knife punctured one of her lungs and the side of her heart. They did emergency surgery and the doctor says she went into a coma. I just came back from there. It's touch and go if the charge will change to murder."

"Could we see the knife?" Ernie asked.

"Sure thing." The chief nodded to Pike who scurried to get it. "Wish we had a full-time forensics lab here but we have to ask the state for help when something happens. They said they'd have someone down here ASAP."

"Not much crime here, Howell?"

"Quiet like a church, Sharyn. And we like it that way."

"I recall another attack here about five years ago," Ernie said. "Wasn't that the same kind of thing? A young woman was killed?"

"Yep. The only two murders we've had hereabouts since 1965. Mostly we get rowdy parties at the college or a boyfriend who won't take no for an answer. Not much happening here. Especially since we don't have much of a full-time population. We have about five thousand with the surrounding county and what the college takes in. Only a couple of hundred right here in town."

Sharyn frowned as she looked at the knife that the officer gave her. It was smeared with dry blood inside the plastic bag.

"Sorry for the mess," Pike said. "We have to keep it like this for the forensics boy."

"I understand." She looked at the carvings on the handle. "This looks old."

"It does," Howell agreed. "And we think those markings might be Cherokee, like Mr. Two Rivers. Might be a family heirloom. Maybe he thought he was attacking a settlement or something. People lose it sometimes."

"The forensics lab won't know what this means either," Ernie remarked, taking the knife from Sharyn. "You'll have to get someone in who understands Cherokee glyphs."

"We had that in mind," Pike answered. "Called someone about it this morning."

"In the meantime, I think we're gonna have to take that old boy down to Morganton and see if a shrink can find out what's wrong with him. I was hoping he'd talk to you and save me a trip."

Pike shook his head. "The way that little girl looked, it'd be enough to drive anybody crazy."

"Have you charged him yet?" Sharyn asked him.

"Not yet. We'd have to take him down to the county seat for that. He don't seem like he's in good shape to travel. I figure we'll let the doctors take a look at him and then see."

"What about that murder five years ago?" she wondered out loud. "Does it match the same MO?"

Howell nodded. "Well, the other girl *was* stabbed. And we did find her here on campus. We never found a suspect or the murder weapon. Pike, check and see if we have those files from that case or if the state boy took them with him."

"Yes, sir!"

"The SBI looked into that one for us since it was a murder and all. They were here for weeks but never could come up with anything." Howell's eyes brightened. "You're thinking that Mr. Two Rivers might be responsible for both?"

That *wasn't* what she was thinking but she could see how it could appear that way to him. "Well, it *could* have been done by the same person. Not necessarily Sam."

Howell looked embarrassed. "I'm sorry, Sharyn. I forgot he's your friend. What did you say he did for you?"

"He works with our wildlife administrator for the county. Mostly he takes care of animals."

"I see."

"I can't find that file, sir. But there's a fax coming in." Pike jumped up to check it. "It's the information we requested on Mr. Two Rivers."

"Well, let's see what it has to say." The chief put on his glasses.

It wasn't good. Sam had been arrested a dozen times in his life. Mostly for animal rights protests. A few times the arrests included assault on the officer who arrested him.

"Looks like he was discharged from the military under less than honorable circumstances too." Howell handed her the sheet. "Assault on an officer. He could've been shot for that during wartime."

"The charges were dropped against him." Sharyn glanced at the sheet. "He was discharged afterwards but with nothing against his record."

"Sounds like your friend has a history of violence." Howell put a pinch of tobacco between his cheek and tooth. He held out the tin to Ernie.

"No, thanks."

Howell laughed. "I'd offer you some, Sharyn, but you don't look the type."

She smiled, not sure how to answer. "Sam wouldn't hurt anyone unless they were doing something to an animal."

"Maybe he lost it. Maybe he thought Miss Ashe was doing something to an animal. It happens. I mean, you thought he'd respond to you. He didn't. Who knows what terrible place he's in right now with that little girl's blood on his hands."

Sharyn had heard enough. "Mind if we have a look around?"

"Not at all. I'd appreciate your help. Diamond Springs gets a lot more crime. I know you all see at least three or four murders a year. Let me know if you see anything we missed. I'm going to process this information and make that call to Morganton. Pike can take you through the way we think it happened."

"Thanks." She held her hand out to him. "I appreciate you letting us look over your shoulder. Sam's a good friend. It's hard for me to believe he did this."

"I enjoyed you being here! I don't get to talk enough about my job, you know? Most people don't want to hear it! And I'm sorry about your friend. But unless something else comes up, that's all she wrote. He'll have to stand trial for hurting Miss Ashe. Knock on wood, it won't turn into murder."

"I know what you mean. I'd appreciate it if you'd keep in touch about this. Sam's friends will want to know what's going on. And if you find that file on the other murder, I'd like to see it."

"I'll do that. It was great to meet you, Sharyn."

"You too, Howell!"

Pike took them out of the tiny police station. The sun was shining fitfully, sailing in and out of the heavy clouds. There was still some frost on the ground and on the stone fence that ran through the town along the edge of the highway. The skeletal trees swayed in the slight breeze making clicking sounds with their branches like they were feeling for their leaves. But it was a long way 'til spring.

Ernie and Sharyn didn't speak as Pike told them about the college and the grounds.

"It was founded in 1865 right after the war. Mr. Elwood Piper lost his only child during the fighting. He decided after it was over to turn the house and all the storage buildings he had into a college. He funded it with his own money for almost thirty years before he died. He created the gardens and the planetarium."

"It's beautiful," Sharyn said as the wind shifted dead leaves across the ground at her feet. "How many students go to school here?"

"Right now, there are about three hundred and fifty. It changes from year to year." He smiled at her. "Where did you go to school, Sheriff?"

"I went to UNC at Chapel Hill. I wanted to be a lawyer."

"On the other side of the blanket, huh?"

"Sometimes it seems that way but we're all part of the legal process."

"Yeah. Just don't like lawyers much, you know?"

Ernie grinned lopsided at her.

"Here's the dorm where Lynette Ashe was staying. We have her room sealed off, but I can take you up there."

"Thanks."

The dorm was a big gray stone building that looked like it could house all 350 people by itself. Downstairs were the kitchen and social areas. Upstairs were the students' rooms. Pike carefully climbed under the tape that sealed off the room at the end of the hall. He held it up for Sharyn as she ducked under it.

"We figure it started here." He showed them the mess that was still in the room. Clothes were everywhere. Lampshades were covered in underwear and a nightgown clothed the tiny television. There was a huge pile of clay-stained athletic socks in one corner.

"Any blood?" Sharyn thought that the room didn't look worse than her dorm at college. Or anyone else's for that matter. She counted at least four laptops and five PDAs. It seemed like a lot of hardware but everyone knew that the girls at the school were rich.

"We couldn't find any but the forensics boys probably will."

She was surprised that he was willing to take them into the crime scene. Nick would kill her if she showed a crime scene to people before he got there.

"Seems like it would be pretty obvious with the kind of wounds your chief described," Ernie considered, walking through the mess.

"We think he grabbed her here then took her outside to kill her."

"Anyone hear any screams?" Sharyn looked out of the window down to the brown lawn.

"No. We think she was probably asleep. He surprised her. Snatched her up and dragged her out before anyone knew what happened to her."

Ernie frowned. "What time was she attacked?"

"About ten P.M."

Sharyn's eyebrows lifted. "That's pretty early. Weren't the halls full of girls?"

"Lights out is at ten. We figure they were all in bed asleep."

"Then what happened?" she continued, not wanting to dwell on the inadequacies of the case.

"Well, sir, we figure he took her outside." Pike matched his words to his deeds taking them back outside the dorm house. "He dragged or carried her down here."

The area where the girl was found was taped off to prevent anyone from entering. Blood covered the ground, staining the leaves and withered grass. It was close to the foundation of the building.

Sharyn stepped back to place the streetlights. There was one in front of the house and one on the other side between dorm houses. The area would've been in complete darkness. "What's that big building over there?"

Pike didn't have to look. "The main building. It holds the library, conference rooms and most of the classes. Everything else is scattered through the other buildings on this side and across the street. Main office in the old Piper house."

"How did you know to look for her here?" Ernie wondered.

"Well, we got a call from someone telling us that something was up," Pike explained. "The chief and I came out with a few deputized citizens. We had dogs and searchlights. We found him kneeling down next to her with the knife in his hand. He almost looked like he was praying over her. Maybe he thought she was dead already and was asking her for forgiveness."

Sharyn considered the scenario he painted for her. She'd seen Sam track a mother bear and her cubs up the mountain. He knew animals and the darkness. Unless they were right and he was crazy, he would've heard them coming from the time they left the police station across the street. He could've been long gone before they thought to look there for him.

"Did the caller pinpoint this area or was it a lucky shot?" Ernie persisted.

Pike grinned. "A lucky shot, I guess. The dogs probably smelled the blood. Doody Frankin's got some good dogs."

Ernie agreed. "Finest dogs around. We've used them ourselves a few times."

"What about Lynette Ashe? Does she have a boyfriend?" Sharyn questioned him.

"I don't think there was much point in checking." Pike laughed. "It's a pretty open and shut case, Sheriff. Unless we can connect Mr. Two Rivers to the other murder, like you said."

Sharyn wanted to bite her tongue. Instead, she looked at him. "And what was his motive?"

"Excuse me?"

"His motive for trying to kill the girl. Why would he want to kill her? Did they know each other?"

Pike studied her like a deer studies a hunter. "Sheriff, I know Mr. Two Rivers is your friend but we caught him redhanded. End of story. All we're lacking is a confession. With that history on him, it makes it complete. He has a background of assaults. The girl probably brushed him off. It's not pretty but it makes a whole picture."

She nodded. She didn't want to alienate the deputy or his boss. "It looks bad for him, Pike. I appreciate you taking us around."

His face brightened at once. "Sure thing, Sheriff! I better get back now. But you all come back in the spring when we have our azalea festival. Now that's a fine time of year!"

He shook both their hands then loped back across the campus towards the highway.

Ernie rasped his hand across his jaw. "I'd say Sam is guilty whether he is or not. They've got him tried and hanged."

"He needs a good lawyer." Sharyn followed the officer's route back to her Jeep.

"A good lawyer like Matlock or Perry Mason!" Ernie ran across the street with her. "Nobody else is gonna get him off!"

"There's not much we can do here, Ernie." She opened the door and the gift fell out again.

This time Ernie was beside her and scooped it up before she could stop him. "Fancy wrapping. Nice card." He read the note inside and looked at her. "You weren't gonna tell me about this?"

She took the box and tossed it into the trashcan at the front of the police office. "What's to tell?"

Ernie got into the Jeep. He stared at her as she started the engine and secured her seatbelt. "What's to tell? Jack Winter is trouble and you know it. Are you encouraging him? Is this some kind of stunt like Kristie getting a job with him? You cozy up to him and he spills his guts?"

"You have good ears," she muttered, thinking back to the party.

"Seriously, Sharyn. You don't want to mess with him. I thought you knew better!"

"Ernie, he left me a gift on my car seat." She didn't tell him that Jack somehow managed to do it *with* her car doors locked. "You make it sound like I asked him out to dinner."

He peered at her carefully. "You didn't, did you?"

"I saw him last night," she explained as they drove back to Diamond Springs. "He said he wanted to come to the party but Mom wouldn't invite him because of Caison. I guess he left me a present later."

"Bless his black heart!"

"Could we worry more about what we're going to do to help Sam? I think I can handle Jack Winter."

Ernie took off his glasses and cleaned them on his shirt. "Let it rest, Sharyn. I know you think he set your mama's house on fire. I know you think he knows something about your daddy. But let it go. It won't bring your daddy back and it might get you buried next to him."

She glanced at him. "You're afraid of him."

"Darn straight! Any sane, rational person would be. The man is a devil."

"I'm not going out of my way to find him. It seems to be the opposite."

Ernie worried his lip with his teeth as he thought about what she said. "I know you've got a good head on your shoulders. Just use it, huh?"

Sharyn knew he meant well. He was like a father to her since T. Raymond died. He was her father's best friend when he was alive. She thought Ernie was the one who would take his place. But Ernie had other plans. He encouraged her to run for sheriff the first time and for re-election. He always told her that he didn't like the limelight that the office required.

"I try. So. What about Sam?"

He looked out of the window as they got closer to Diamond Springs. "I don't know. If he won't speak up, they might convict him with diminished capacity."

"He spoke to us when we first got there. Do you think he felt like they were watching us?"

"Maybe. Sam's wily. I know you had to be thinking the same thing I was back there. He would've known they were coming two weeks ago and been gone before they knew it happened."

"Like you said, if someone doesn't figure out what happened, he'll end up in jail or the mental ward at Morganton."

Ernie scratched his head. "I don't know. What are our options?"

"We get Nick to offer to do the forensic work to speed things up. And we investigate on the side."

"And behind the chief's back?"

She laughed. "Something like that."

"We could do what we can with the computer first, I guess. Check out what there is about Lynette Ashe. Maybe there's some correlation besides Sam."

"I knew you'd think of something."

"And when are we going to find time to catch up with the Silver Dollar Gang?"

Sharyn pulled the Jeep into the back parking lot at the sheriff's office. She swung into her usual parking spot and turned off the engine. "Who needs sleep?"

"No!" Nick was emphatic. "I'm not going to do forensic work in Rock Springs!"

"Nick—"

"Sharyn, I mean it! I'm not done processing the prints and evidence from the house burglaries. I still have some left over from the first one. There's only so much of me to go around."

She sat down in his office in the dank basement of the Diamond Springs' hospital. "Sam will probably be convicted of hurting this girl unless we help him."

"Maybe he hurt her. Did you ever think about that?" He struggled with a pile of reports. "You said he was unresponsive. Where's his lawyer anyway?"

"He doesn't have one yet."

"Sounds like you should be talking to a lawyer instead of a medical examiner!"

"Nick, the only ME is from the state forensics lab. He travels around to little spots like Rock Springs and does what he can. He isn't looking for evidence to prove who did it. He's looking for evidence to prove Sam did it so he can go on to the next town."

He stopped trying to shove the papers into his briefcase. "I can't do it. Even if you did all the paperwork I have here from the robberies. I can't use the kids on it either. The dean complained about me taking them out with me at all times of the day and night. It seems some parent didn't think it was a good idea for their child to be exposed to dead people and crime."

She slumped in her chair, forgetting about Sam for a moment. "What are you going to do?"

He waved a document in the air. "Hire two full-time assistants."

"You got the money from the commission to hire people?"

"Yep! And some left over for new equipment. They said my services were important to the county and gave me a pat on the back and a raise for everything I do for them."

"Wow! I need to make an appointment to talk to them about the sheriff's office!"

"They were in a pretty good mood yesterday. Or it helps that Reed Harker is gone. I don't know which."

"You flirted with Julia, didn't you?" she accused with a smile.

"I didn't have to. Not that I wouldn't have to get the money. I'm going to hire Megan and Keith. They've been with me the longest and they both want to pursue this as a career. The dean won't be able to say anything about what they do outside of school."

"That's great. So, you *would* have help to work on Sam's case."

Nick managed to close his briefcase. It bulged at the sides but the clasps snapped shut. "Unlike you, I need time to sleep and eat. Come back after we solve the robberies and we'll talk."

Her pager went off. "Probably another robbery."

"I have to get to class anyway."

She kissed his cheek and smiled at him. "I'll talk to you later."

He sighed and kissed her lips. "Fine! I can't take the torture. I'll look at Sam's stuff. *If* they'll let me! If they have their heart set on a state guy doing, it, they might not be happy with me."

"Thanks, Nick! You're the best!" She hugged him.

"Is there something I should know about Sam that you're not telling me? It's not like you to get involved in things outside the county."

"He's a friend. He's being railroaded. And he's dating Aunt Selma."

He slapped his head with the palm of his hand. "Why didn't

you say so to begin with? I'd stay up all night and all day rather than face the wrath of Aunt Selma!"

Her pager went off again. "I have to go. Would you like me to call Chief Murray in Rock Springs?"

"No." He lifted the briefcase with difficulty. "I don't want him to know that I couldn't resist the sheriff's big blue eyes. I'd rather lie and say I'm looking for something else to do because there's never enough going on here to keep me busy."

She kissed him again quickly then left him to wrestle his briefcase to his classroom.

"Wrap it up," Ernie instructed Cari as they stood inside another house that had been robbed. "Nobody goes in or out until we know if it was the Silver Dollar Gang."

"Another robbery?" Sharyn asked him as she joined them.

He glanced at her. "Oh! It's the sheriff! Where were you?"

"Asking Nick to take a look at the forensics in Sam's assault case."

"Is he gonna do it?"

"Yes. He said he didn't have anything better to do and eating and sleeping meant nothing to him." She grinned at him.

Ernie snorted. "I bet he did!"

"What's going on here?"

"Another robbery. Looks the same as the other ones to me. The family is out of town. The house had an alarm. The thieves took it offline then opened the lock and went inside. Just as pretty and smooth as a quiet lake."

"There has to be some way to track them. Let's do a pattern of their hits and see what we come up with. I know we've looked at all the people involved for clues. Let's look at the places."

"Sounds like a plan." He glanced up. "Oh-oh. Here comes trouble!"

Sharyn watched the approaching news vans and straightened her shoulders. "I'll talk to them. Close up here and see what you can do with that geography idea."

"You got it, Sheriff. What about Sam's case?"

"I don't know. You and Cari work on this. I'll check out Lynette Ashe when I get back to the office."

"Okay. What are you gonna say to the vultures?"

"I'll think of something."

"Sheriff, is this another break-in like the last one?" a reporter called to her as he walked across the wet grass. "Is it the Silver Dollar Gang?"

"I don't know yet," she answered. "I can't tell you the differences. That would be giving our case away."

"So there *is* a case?" Foster Odom, the head reporter for the Diamond Springs' Gazette demanded. "I mean, it looks like the sheriff's office is spinning its wheels."

"There *is* a case and we're collecting evidence, Mr. Odom. When we have something else we can tell you, we will."

"What about the rumor that the commission might be creating a separate police force for Diamond Springs?"

"I haven't heard about that yet." She justified the lie in her mind by qualifying it. She didn't hear about it from the commission yet. "And I have to go. Thanks for coming out."

Her cell phone went off as she got back in her Jeep. "Sheriff Howard."

"Sheriff? This is Howell Murray. We just got Sam Two Rivers installed here at Morganton. They'll be looking at him for the next forty-eight hours to determine his state of mind. I got the go ahead from the county DA to charge him. Assault with a deadly weapon. Unless they keep him here, we'll be moving him to the county jail to wait for his trial."

She digested the information. "Thanks, Howell. I appreciate you keeping me up to date on this."

"I heard from your ME over there, Nick Thomo-Thomo—"

"Thomopolis?"

"Yeah. I knew it was something Greek sounding. He offered to come over and do our forensics on Mr. Two River's case. I told him we'd be glad to have him. Except for one thing."

"What's that, Howell?"

"I'm afraid that people in your county might be too willing to look the other way on this since Mr. Two Rivers is your friend and he's worked with the county and all. I've heard tell that Nick is a darn good man but I think we'll wait for the state ME. He called and said he was prioritizing our case so he'll be out tomorrow. We should know something then."

"Okay. Keep me posted."

"You got it!"

Sharyn closed her cell phone and drove back towards town. Nick called and repeated what Howell told her. He said Megan and Keith accepted his offers of full-time jobs with the county. "I'm glad."

"I'm sorry it didn't work out about Sam."

"Me too. We'll have to do the best we can with the state ME."

"I have class. I'll talk to you later."

Selma Howard was waiting for her niece at the door to the sheriff's office. "What did you find out?"

"Come inside," Sharyn said. "I don't want to talk out here."

In her office, Sharyn explained what happened in Rock Springs. "We couldn't do anything to stop them from taking him to Morganton but it may be a blessing."

"How?"

"Well, he won't be charged for forty-eight hours. All we have to do is find the person who really hurt that girl in that time and Sam will be cleared."

Selma groaned. "What's the likelihood of that?"

"I don't know. We need to find out all the information we can on Lynette Ashe. Her boyfriend, girlfriends, family. We need to know her habits. And we need to check any links to another girl who was killed at Piper five years ago. Apparently, the murder was similar to this assault. This one was interrupted. Maybe Sam saw it happening and stopped it."

Selma brightened. "I can do that. I have a computer at the

school and I can ask around about Lynette. I didn't know her personally but I've heard the students talking about her. Does the police chief think the same person did both crimes?"

Sharyn sighed. "He does now."

"All right. So Sam needs an alibi for the murder five years ago too?"

"Exactly. And we'll have to hope in the meantime that Lynette comes to and can identify who attacked her."

Selma stood up and wrapped her chenille shawl around her. "Anything else?"

"That's it except for one thing. What if we find out Sam *is* guilty?"

"We won't. I can tell things about people, Sharyn. You know that. Sam is a good man. He didn't hurt this girl or the one five years ago. We just have to prove it."

Sharyn hugged her aunt. "Good luck. Let me know what you find out."

"I'll call you," Selma promised. "Thank you, Sharyn. You know it's been a long time between dates for me."

"I know. This was unexpected. But I'm happy for you."

"I guess I'll need to start wearing black." Selma took a moment to consider her wardrobe.

"Black?" Sharyn wondered with a smile.

"You know, so I can spy on people and not be seen at night. Cloak and dagger. Really, Sharyn! I thought you understood what it's like to go undercover!"

Ernie was standing at her door ready to knock when Selma came out and headed for the back door without saying a word to him. "She's upset over Sam?"

"Nope. She's going undercover at the college to find out what happened." Sharyn laughed. "I hope I didn't unleash more than the place can handle."

Ernie whistled. "I hope not too! But I've got something for you on those break-ins. Maybe they're not as smart as they think they are!"

Chapter Four

"When we put all of the burglaries on the map, we come up with this grid." Ernie punched it on the computer. The houses that were robbed showed up as red dots on the map of Montgomery County.

"All of the them on the east side of the county," Cari added.

Sharyn looked at the map: "Our lowest crime and lowest population area."

"And the fastest growing area in the county."

"What *was* our lowest crime area anyway. All of them were newer houses with alarm systems. All of the locks were picked after the alarm was turned off. Nothing broken or out of place except what they took. They always take the same basic items. Jewelry, cash, and electronic items that are easy to carry and to get rid of. We know from their shoe prints that there's probably four or five of them. They all wear the same shoes. Nikes. Size twelve. They wear gloves and probably something on their heads because we haven't been able to find any hair samples either."

Cari continued when Ernie paused for breath, "They travel together in a Chevy van. We know that from the tire prints. No description of the van yet."

"Well, that didn't make a lot of difference, did it?" Sharyn was disappointed with the results.

Ernie disagreed. "We know the basic area they're working. Maybe we could set something up."

"We could set up a house for them to rob and monitor it." Sharyn warmed to the idea. "They'd come in thinking it was like any other house and we'd have them on tape!"

"It could work," Cari agreed. "I'd like to have a chance to kick their—"

"Okay Cari," Ernie advised. "Let's get the video equipment out of storage and canvas the area. We'll have to find someone willing to go along with the idea of having their house broken into."

"Good idea. Last resort, we could set the house up from an empty one that a builder is trying to sell. Since we know the group checks everything out before they rob the house, it would be better the other way. See what you can find."

"We're on it!" Cari pulled on her gloves and hat.

Ernie sighed and rolled his eyes.

"Where's Joe and Ed?" Sharyn asked Trudy.

"Out rounding up a rabid raccoon near Frog Meadow," the office manager replied as she answered the phone. "Line one, Sheriff. It's Nick."

"I'll take it in my office." Sharyn ignored Marvella's anguished sigh as she sat at her desk in the outer office compiling reports on the break-ins.

"Sharyn, I think I have something for you on the robberies," Nick began without preliminary. "I found a strand of hair at the last one on Diamond Crescent Road. It's a long, blond strand. And a thumbprint that doesn't belong to either of the people who live there."

"That's great! Do we know if the hair belongs to anyone who lives in the house?"

"Would I call you without checking that out? The two people who live there, Marcia and Blair Stuckey, have short brown hair. I have copies of their prints already. They don't match the one I found. I think one of our thieves got careless."

"Any takers on who it belongs to?"

"Not yet but I have it running through the data bases. I sent the hair strand off to Raleigh for DNA, and that might take a while."

"Thanks, Nick."

"Anything on Sam yet?"

"They're holding him at Morganton for forty-eight hours before they charge him. Aunt Selma is doing some research."

"Is that a good idea?"

She laughed. "I'll let you know."

Marvella knocked at her office door as Sharyn hung up the phone. "Sheriff? I need to know what to do to make this right with Ernie."

Sharyn sat down at her desk. "I don't think it's personal, Marvella."

"It sounds personal to me!" Marvella took one of the chairs opposite her. "He told me this morning that I couldn't wear my purple scarf around my neck when I was wearing my uniform!"

"I know you hate the brown but he's right. We're not supposed to wear scarves or lots of jewelry or flowered hats. We're the law enforcement for this county. We have to be able to walk up to a car that we've pulled over for speeding and demand respect."

Marvella was unimpressed. "He didn't say anything about Cari wearing those black leather gloves or Joe wearing his shades all the time! Ernie hates me since I went against him. I might as well quit now."

"He doesn't hate you," Sharyn said. "He wants you to be the best deputy you can. He's been training deputies for ten years. He knows what he's doing. And he's seen lots worse than you."

"You mean David?" Marvella laughed. "Honey, I know that's true!"

Sharyn wasn't going there. "Don't give up yet. It's only been a couple of weeks."

"All right. I'll do my best. Maybe with all this other stuff he'll forget about me. Otherwise, I don't know if I can handle the stress. This is a stressful job all by itself!"

"I know. Thanks for sticking it out, Marvella. It gets easier."

"I'm only doin' it for you. It sure isn't for the money! I've always had a good feeling about you, Sheriff. I know I can do important things here with you."

"Thanks. I know you can too!" The phone rang again. "Sheriff Howard."

It was Selma. "You need to come down here! I think I found something important!"

"I'll be there as soon as I can." Sharyn picked up her gun and hat after she hung up the phone. "I have to go, Marvella. It takes time to work into an established unit. Trust me. I know about that. Trudy, I'll be out of the office for a while."

"I'll call if anything comes up. Your mother called and wants you to bring home a quart of milk tonight."

She grimaced. "Thanks, Trudy!"

Sharyn drove into Rock Springs a little after noon. The streets were crowded with students walking from class to class. She found the building where her aunt was teaching and parked in front of it. The building was small, not much more than the size of a house. It was two stories of gray stone that was weathered from the hot Carolina sun and cold wet winters. Ivy grew up one side and across some of the wide porch that was set with rockers.

Selma met her at the front door. "Sharyn, I've spoken with some of Lynette's friends. They say she didn't have a boyfriend right now because she recently broke up with a boy. They say he wasn't very happy about it either. And she broke up with him because he had a temper."

Sharyn was impressed. "Who is he?"

"His name is Tim Stryker. He lives in Diamond Springs. I thought it would be easier for you to question him there instead of me luring him here on a ruse to speak with him. That way, he won't suspect anything."

"Tim Stryker?" Sharyn took out her notebook. "I know him. He was involved in Carrie Sommer's murder. He's the boy who brought the gun into the sheriff's office."

"So he *is* a little wild and has a temper!" Selma nodded knowingly. "He's probably the one who did it!"

"Maybe. What else did you find out?"

Selma beckoned her niece into her office that sat at the front of the building. She closed the door carefully behind her. "I don't want anyone to know I'm looking for the attacker."

"Aunt Selma, you've been involved with law enforcement officers all of your life. How can you be so . . . dramatic about it?"

"Dramatic?" She drew herself up. "I don't know what you mean! I'm being careful! Anyway, I looked up everything I could about Lynette. I did a print out of it." She handed Sharyn the paper.

Sharyn gave up trying to understand why her aunt was acting like a detective on TV and glanced over the paper. "Her parents are out of the country?"

"In Switzerland. They're both surgeons."

"That's tough. I hope they get back in case she doesn't make it."

"I hope so too, poor thing. But they can't be involved. She doesn't have any siblings. I listed the girls in her dorm that she spends time with. She's a good student. No financial problems. I couldn't find anything out of the ordinary about her. *Except* for Tim Stryker."

"He has that effect on people." Sharyn recalled how Carrie Sommer's family felt about him after their daughter was killed. "What about teachers here on campus? Clubs?"

"I couldn't find any club affiliations," Selma reported, putting on her glasses. "I listed her subjects and teachers. She's just your average student. Except for—"

"Tim Stryker." Sharyn acknowledged. "I know."

"What do you think?" Selma whispered.

"I think I'll talk to Tim and see if he has an alibi."

"Should I say something to Chief Murray?"

"Not yet. We don't have anything to say yet. I hate to keep him out in the cold but he's convinced Sam did this. We have to give him a reason to doubt himself."

Selma took off her glasses. "I got him a lawyer. Jill

Madison-Farmer agreed to take the case. I like her. I think she'll do a good job."

"Have you called his family in Cherokee? I don't know if the chief contacted them but they should know what's happening."

"No. I don't know who his kin are. Sam mentions them once in a while but not often. I don't think they get along much."

"His brother is the sheriff up there. I'll give him a call later and let him know. Maybe he can throw some weight behind another investigation too."

Selma hugged her. "Thank you, Sharyn. I'm glad Kristie is back at school. Otherwise I'd be worried about leaving her alone too much. I know she needed me for a while but I thinks she's okay now."

"Did she tell you her plan to work for Jack Winter and spy on him?" Sharyn wondered if Selma knew about it.

"No!" Her aunt was astonished. "You can't think I'd agree to such a fool thing! I'll talk to her."

"Thanks. She'll probably be mad that I told you. But I don't like her thinking she can help me like that." Sharyn looked out the window. "It's not raining anymore. Let's take a walk across campus. I'd like to see the whole layout."

They followed the gravel paths that went from building to building along the campus. The brown grass was wet and spongy from all the rain. Selma's building was closest to the main office.

"Impressive." Sharyn looked up at the four huge pillars holding up the front entrance.

The portico was ornate almost to the point of being gaudy with scrollwork leaves and flowers. There was a wide set of double doors that led inside across a white porch set with rocking chairs. Purple and pink pansies struggled in the cold breezes between 200-year-old oaks that guarded the three-story house.

"I think Mr. Elwood Piper was somewhat of a maverick. This college was one of the first set up as an all girls' school.

It was almost unheard of in its day. You have to admire a man who thought women should be educated in a time when most weren't." Selma put her gloved hand on the cold statue of Elwood Piper.

"Officer Kaiser said the rest of the buildings were originally storehouses?"

"And slaves' quarters. Except for the big main building across the street. That was built later. I went to school here, you know. I graduated in 1965."

That date rang a bell in Sharyn's mind. "Chief Murray said there was another murder here that year."

Selma considered it. "I remember. Yes. They almost closed the college. I was so worried that I wouldn't graduate in June. That was a long time ago. I almost forgot about it."

Sharyn smiled. She could only imagine her aunt that long ago. The rain began falling again. The temperature dropped as they walked past Lynette Ashe's dorm house. "You know, there's a lot about this that doesn't make any sense."

"Does killing ever make sense?"

"Yes. I'm afraid it does. It makes sense to the one who did it. It might not be what we would consider sense but they do."

"Oh, look!" Selma pointed to a man who was approaching them. He was in a wheelchair but the wide tires were speeding down the worn gravel path. "Professor Neal!"

He stopped abruptly as he reached them. "Miss Howard."

"Professor, this is my niece, Sharyn. She's the sheriff of Diamond Springs. Sharyn, this is Professor Aaron Neal. He's taught here at this school since it opened."

Professor Neal laughed heartily. "I'm not quite that old but I have been here a very long time." He held out his hand to Sharyn.

She grasped his cold hand in hers. "I don't think any of us should be out in this weather unless we want whatever strain of flu is going around."

"You're right, Sheriff," Professor Neal agreed. "Please, the two of you come over to my office. I left some tea brewing before I went out."

"Thanks but I have to get back," Sharyn said regretfully. "Maybe I could have a rain check on that?"

"Of course, you're welcome anytime! Are you investigating the attack on poor Lynette?"

"Not officially, sir. Was she a student of yours?"

"Yes. A bright, capable girl. What a tragedy! I hope she pulls through. I'm sure the chief can use all the help he can get. How about you Selma, tea?"

"Yes, please! I'll call you later, Sharyn. I'll be looking into that other . . . thing we were talking about."

"Okay. Nice meeting you, Professor."

"You too, Sheriff. Good luck with the case."

"Thanks."

Pike Kaiser hailed her as she was walking back to her Jeep. "Sheriff? What brings you out here today? Didn't Chief Murray tell you that your friend is in Morganton?"

"Yes." She turned to face him. "My aunt is working here for a semester. I was talking to her."

"Oh really?" He looked back towards Selma and Professor Neal. "What's she teach?"

"Herbology. She's been a herbalist since I was a little girl."

"That's nice." He grinned but his tone was patronizing. "You know, you have a reputation for not being satisfied with the truth."

Sharyn studied him. "Really? That might be a reputation for *finding* the truth despite what people think is right or wrong."

"Whatever. We're handling this case. You don't have any call to be involved."

"I told you, Officer Kaiser. I was here visiting my aunt. I don't want to handle this case. I have plenty to do in Diamond Springs."

"Good. Just so we understand each other."

"Just so *you* handle the case and not jump to assumptions on everything you find!" She nodded to him and walked away.

She half expected him to follow her. He didn't. He stood watching her as she backed the Jeep out of the parking area.

There was something faintly creepy about this place. She remembered her aunt asking her if she wanted to go to college there when she was in high school. She said no so quickly that her father laughed. But the place made her uneasy. The large dark red stain on the earth surrounded by yellow police tape flapping in the breeze did nothing to lessen the impression.

She called Jefferson Two Rivers right away. He was out of the office. She left a message for him to call her. She didn't know how Sam would feel about her calling his brother but there was no way to ask him. To her mind, what was happening constituted an emergency. That meant notifying next of kin.

Ernie called her when she was almost in Diamond Springs. "I have some news for you. You're not gonna like it and I partially blame myself for it happening. I thought you should know before you get back."

She was more disturbed by the tone of his voice than his words. "What is it?"

"Someone found your gift from Jack Winter in the trash outside the Rock Springs' police station. It was a watch shaped like a heart. Apparently, there was an inscription and a note inside the box with it."

"How do you know?"

"The person who found it gave it to WXLZ. They've been having a field day with it on the radio all afternoon."

She swallowed hard. "What did the note say?"

"I know in my heart that we were meant to be together." The inscription on the watch is *Love is forever."*

"Fantastic."

"Exactly. Stay away from the front of the building. Reporters are everywhere."

She hung up the phone thoughtfully. How bad could it be?

She had her answer a few minutes after getting back. Trudy was frantically answering the phone, telling reporters that she would take their names and numbers. Reporters were waiting patiently in the rain in front of the sheriff's office. They pasted their faces against the glass trying to peer into the building. Ernie and Cari were watching television as the local cable channel that usually carried school menus talked about the romance between the sheriff and the senator.

Ernie looked up as Sharyn took off her hat. "I'm sorry, ma'am."

"It's not your fault, Ernie." She shook the rain from her curly hair and brushed it from her shoulders. "I shouldn't have handled it that way."

Marvella looked up from her growing stack of papers. "Don't let them bandy you around like that! You got a right to see who ever you want!"

"I'm not seeing him, Marvella. This is all on his side."

Marvella's mouth made a round O then she looked back at her paperwork.

"Your mother's on line one, Sheriff," Trudy said. "If we don't do something, the lines are going to explode!"

Sharyn picked up the phone. "Hi Mom."

"I can't believe you didn't tell me! Did you think I wouldn't be happy for you? No wonder you were so miserable when you thought I was dating him. It explains a lot of his actions towards you too."

Sharyn really didn't want to know what she meant by that. "I have to go, Mom. Sorry. We'll talk about it later."

"What do you want me to say to them?" Ernie asked her.

"Nothing."

"Oh, you have to say something!" Marvella found her voice again. "What you say now will either stoke up the fire or put it out! I'd say from the look on your face that you want to put it out."

"What do you suggest?"

Marvella got up quickly from her desk. "You leave it to me!"

Ernie, Sharyn and Cari watched as Marvella went outside and addressed the crowd. They didn't hear what she said to them but the reporters started moving away from the door.

They packed up their gear and headed back to their cars and vans.

"What did you say?" Ernie asked her when she came back inside.

"I said that they weren't going to get anything standing out there but pneumonia! I told them that the sheriff would have a press conference when she was ready and that anyone who wanted to come would have to clear out in the next five minutes!"

"That was great, Marvella!" Sharyn enthused. "We might have to appoint you as the spokesperson for the department."

"Is there a pay raise in that?" Marvella checked.

"Nope." Ernie dashed her dreams. "And you don't get to shoot a gun any quicker either."

Ed came in the back door. "Sheriff? You have to talk to him."

Joe followed him. His uniform was slashed and full of blood on his right leg.

"What happened?" Sharyn asked seeing the wound.

"The rabid raccoon either bit him or slashed at him. He won't go to the hospital."

Joe winced. "I'll wash it out with peroxide."

"You'll have to get rabies shots, son."

"I'm not getting rabies shots, Ernie."

"You don't have any choice," Ed told him. "Otherwise you could die from rabies."

Sharyn agreed. "You might as well go on to the hospital, Joe. They aren't as bad as they used to be but you're going to be out for a few weeks."

Joe removed his sunglasses. "Sheriff, you know I've gone along with this even though I thought it wasn't right to have trained deputies catching wild animals. If I have to get rabies shots, I'm quitting. That's it."

The TV blared in the background with Trudy trying to tone down her responses on the phone so she could listen.

"That isn't my call, Joe. But I know you have to do this.

You could die from rabies. I'd rather lose you as a deputy than have you die."

He slowly put on his sunglasses then took the deputy's badge from his shirt. He laid it on the desk beside her. "I'm going to change then I'll go to the hospital. I'll come back for my things later."

Ed ran his hand across his face. "I'll drive you."

Joe nodded then disappeared behind the locker room door.

"Isn't there something to say to him?" Ed whispered, glancing at the door.

"He'll change his mind when it's over," Ernie answered. "He'll be fine."

"Except that he's right," Sharyn said. "I've let this go on too long. I'm going to demand that they reinstate the animal control division. We aren't animal catchers. We're law enforcement."

Everyone watched her go into her office and close the door.

"What's going on with the press?" Ed asked in a softer voice.

"It's a long story but they linked the sheriff with Jack Winter," Marvella told him. "She's not too happy about it."

Ed frowned. "What else can go wrong?"

"Don't ask," Ernie advised.

Sharyn answered her phone after calling to demand time at the next commission meeting to address the issue of animal control in the county. The commission secretary gave her five minutes on Thursday morning. There was no use arguing with her. Her argument was with the commission.

Jefferson Two Rivers was on the phone. "Did you say Sam is being held for assault on a girl?"

"Yes. He hasn't been officially arrested yet. He's unresponsive so they took him to Morganton for observation. They plan to arrest him when they release him. I thought you should know."

"Thank you, Sheriff Howard. How's the case against him?"

"Weak but realistic." She lined it up for him. "I don't know how to ask you this but does Sam have a problem?"

"You mean a mental problem?"

"Well, yes."

"Not besides being too stubborn for his own good. If he's not talking it's because he doesn't want to. I'll go and see him. Why didn't the sheriff in Rock Springs call me?"

"I don't think he knew. Sam fought them when they took him in. He's a little messed up. He said a word to my deputy and I when we went to see him. *S-gi-na*. Do you know what he was talking about?"

"*S-gi-na* is a bad spirit, a bad omen. Maybe he was trying to warn you. What did you say the police chief's name is?"

She told him and gave him the number there. "You probably don't know this either but my aunt and Sam have been . . . dating . . . for a little while. She hired a lawyer for him. A local woman. If there's someone you'd rather have—"

"No. That's fine. The best thing would be not to let it get that far. Do you have any ideas, Sheriff?"

"No, sir. I wish I did. I'm checking into some other leads but I don't have anything to help him yet. You're welcome to take over."

"I wish I could but I'm in court on a murder case all this week. I can't get out of it. I'll see if I can get Sam to talk. He must know what happened."

"All right. I will do the best I can to work through it before the arraignment. If not . . . ."

"We'll have to hope your lawyer friend is competent. Please keep me posted, Sheriff."

She told him that she would, then hung up the phone. It rang again and she picked it up. "Sheriff Howard."

"So, I've changed my mind. Being the sheriff's *jilted* boyfriend isn't much fun. Were you going to tell me about Jack before or after we picked out the china?"

"Nick, you know it isn't true!"

"Sharyn, all I know is that things have been strange between you and Jack for a while. Just answer me one question."

"Okay."

"Have you made *him* dinner yet? Or just popcorn?"

She laughed shakily. "You didn't really believe it, did you?"

"I'm not *that* insecure! Although I can see where he could be infatuated with *you*. Besides, I know you don't have time for him. If you arrest him, I might be jealous."

She sat down at her desk and told him what happened. "It was stupid. I didn't think about anyone finding the gift and doing something with it."

"I'm more worried about him stalking you outside your apartment."

"He wasn't stalking me. Just waiting, I guess."

"And he put the gift into your Jeep with the doors locked? I'd say he's paying you back for breaking into his house last year."

"I don't know. This will blow over. I'm sorry you have to go through it too."

"It's my own fault. I wanted people to know that we were dating. You're a high-risk date. I figure people are either going to want to shoot at me when I'm with you or pair you up with evil senators."

"I'm glad you're okay with it."

"I'm not really. Oh, the real reason I called was to tell you that I went out to the new break-in today while you were gone. I found another blond hair. No more thumbprints. Megan says it belongs to a woman."

"How can she tell?"

"She says its Clairol Sunny Blond number three."

Sharyn thought about it. "It could still be a man. Hair coloring isn't limited to women."

He laughed. "I'll tell her. Hey, you wouldn't be interested in an assistant pathologist's job would you?"

"Would you fire Megan for me?"

"In a heartbeat!"

"You're so sweet!"

"Don't worry about the thing with Jack," Nick reassured

her. "If I know him, he won't like it either. I think he wants to lust after you alone in the dark."

She shivered. "Thanks for that picture! I have to go. I'm going to question Tim Stryker about the attack in Rock Springs."

"Who?"

She explained who he was. "Unofficially, of course."

"Of course. Call me when you're through. Maybe we can do dinner or something."

"You aren't nervous about being seen in public with me?"

"Sweetheart, I worked too long and too hard to be with you to care if people think you're letting me down easy. As long as you say we're okay, that's all I care about. Give me a call when you're through."

She smiled. "I will. 'Bye, Nick."

Ernie knocked on the door before he walked into her office. "You've got that moony-eyed look on your face like you just talked to Nick."

"Don't even go there," she warned, continuing to pack her book bag.

"Getting ready to leave?"

"Yes. Then I'm going to talk to Tim Stryker. He's living out at the Cliff's apartments off the Interstate according to the phone book. Selma thinks he probably attacked Lynette."

"That boy gets into more trouble. I'm leaving too. I'll go with you."

"Thanks. How's the house set up going?"

"No takers yet but we're going to try again tomorrow. We might have to use an empty house and set it up ourselves."

She closed her book bag. "Whatever we have to do. I don't want to be working this case next month."

He laughed. "Me either. I want to go away for my honeymoon in peace."

"Where are you going?"

"To Hawaii. That's where Annie's always wanted to go. And since I'm selling my house to move in with her, I could afford it."

"Sounds nice."

"It will be. If we live through the wedding."

Trudy hailed Sharyn as she was leaving. "I heard from Ed. They're keeping Joe overnight for observation then starting his shots tomorrow."

"Thanks. Let's send flowers, huh?"

"One step ahead of you, Sheriff. They're on their way. You owe me twenty dollars."

Sharyn hefted her backpack on her shoulder as she walked out the back door. "You know, a person could go broke sending flowers to people."

"Don't I know it," Ernie agreed.

"You know we're going to have to talk about Marvella, right?"

He put on his hat. "I know."

"How do you want to do it?"

"I'll tell her that we're speeding up her training because of Joe getting hurt. It'll be okay."

They left the parking lot and joined in the early evening traffic going out of town.

"How'd Nick take the press about you and Jack?" He glanced at her as she turned to go to the Interstate.

"He was okay with it, I think. I wish I was."

"It'll blow over."

She frowned as she pulled off the Interstate towards the apartment complex where Tim Stryker lived. "I'm not handling him well, Ernie. I let him get to me. It's like my brain shuts down when I think about him."

"There *isn't* anything between you, is there?"

She shuddered. "Not like you're saying. But he makes me so mad that I feel like I have to find a way to beat him. I'm afraid it makes me do stupid things. Like this with the gift."

"Don't worry about it. He'll get tired of it now that he's in Raleigh. There's bound to be another game he can play."

"I hope so." She looked for a parking place. "Let's get this over with, huh?"

Chapter Five

Tim Stryker was as wild-eyed and messed up as ever. But he had an alibi for his time the night Lynette was hurt. "I'm working down at the old theater. I'm starring as Hamlet. We were working on the sets all night. Ask anyone."

Sharyn nodded. "I will. Thanks, Tim. I hope you're keeping your head down."

He rubbed his bare chest. "I'm working on my craft now, Sheriff. I might go to Hollywood next or New York. I need a good agent. I hate what happened with Lynette but I was ready to move on. I don't care what her friends say."

"All right." She put out her hand. "Good luck then. Please don't go anywhere to work on your craft until this is over."

"I won't. Hamlet runs for a month. Thanks, Sheriff."

"Two murders with him as a suspect," Ernie said as they were leaving the apartment. "He's only what, twenty? Twenty-one? I hope he makes it to New York!"

"That shoots the only other lead we have so far about someone other than Sam attacking Lynette. It was the only thing Selma could find about the girl that looked suspicious."

"What about that murder from five years ago?"

She glanced at him. "I haven't looked into it yet. I'll check it out tonight at home. I don't want to do much of this on county time."

"I'd like to help but I'm going to the caterers with Annie tonight. Then to the restaurant where we're having the re-

66

hearsal dinner. And should I remind you that it's the best man who throws the bachelor party for the groom?"

"Oh great." She pulled the Jeep up into his drive. "You mean girls jumping out of cakes and dirty movies?"

He grinned. "Exactly! I sure don't want to do any of that stuff they're doing at the bridal shower! Oohing and ahhing over Annie's ring and talking about toasters. You're coming to the rehearsal dinner, right?"

"Next Wednesday. I'll be there."

"Good. Thanks, Sharyn. If I have any time left over, I'll check out what I can find about Rock Springs."

"Don't worry about it! Annie will have my head if she thinks you aren't concentrating on the wedding like you're supposed to!"

He laughed. "Not before she has mine! I'll talk to you tomorrow."

Sharyn called Nick on her cell phone. "I'm finished. Are you?"

"No. I'm giving make-up tests. I forgot. You want to bring a pizza over and we'll eat it here while I grade the tests?"

"You always think of such romantic things to do."

Twenty minutes later, she walked into Nick's office at Diamond Springs College with a pizza box balanced on her laptop. The students were filing out after finishing their tests.

"What, no root beer?" he asked when he saw her.

She set down the box and produced two bottles of A&W root beer from her pockets. "Voila!"

"A woman who knows how to shoot a gun and can carry root beer in her pockets," he admired. "No wonder Jack loves you."

"Don't start." She drew up a chair to the side of his cluttered desk and plugged her computer into the extra line on the floor. "Do you ever clean any of this off?"

"Only when it falls on the floor and I have to pick it up. What are you doing?"

"Trying to prove that Sam is innocent of assaulting that girl.

Thanks for trying to look at the evidence anyway. The chief doesn't trust us to be fair and impartial."

He picked up a piece of pizza. "I wonder why?"

She shook her head as she set up her laptop. "I don't know. And his assistant is getting aggressive about it."

"You mean he doesn't want you snooping behind them?"

"You could say that."

He smiled. "So you're snooping behind him more carefully?"

"Exactly."

"What are you looking up in the computer?"

She bit into a piece of pizza. The cheese was stringy. As she pulled, it fell off and dropped down on her chin. Her face flaming red with embarrassment, she picked up a napkin and wiped it off. It didn't help that Nick continued to watch her with a big grin plastered on his face. "You could look away!"

"Why? You look so cute covered in pizza sauce!"

"I'm so sure!"

"I'll bet even the chief in Rock Springs would think so!"

Deliberately, she took some pizza sauce on her finger and put it on the tip of his nose. "There. Now you can look cute too!"

He opened his root beer. "I'll bet you'd look cute in root beer foam too!"

"Nick!"

"Okay. Okay." He wiped the pizza sauce from his nose with a napkin. "Is it safe to ask the question again?"

Sharyn put down her pizza. "I'm looking at the murder that happened there five years ago. I thought there might be something there that could help me with this attack. Both attacks were done with a knife. This one was interrupted. Maybe there's some relationship besides Sam."

"Are you sure Sam can't be held for both of them?"

She told him about her slip suggesting that aspect to the chief.

He shrugged. "Well you're used to looking *for* those things, not trying to go the other way."

"The chief couldn't find his file on the case but I thought there might be something in the newspapers. Hopefully something that puts the two attacks together without Sam being involved. Otherwise, I don't have any other avenues to pursue."

"I know you like Sam. But he might be guilty."

"He might be," she agreed. "But it doesn't sound like him. Although the chief found other assaults he was arrested for, and he was drummed out of the army under less than honorable conditions. His brother is going to see him. Maybe he can get him to talk and we'll know more."

"I don't know him well," Nick said, finishing his pizza. "But if there's anything else I can do, let me know."

"Anything on that thumbprint yet?"

"Not yet. I've gone through all the criminal and military data banks. Nothing."

"What's left?"

"Children who've been printed in case of kidnapping. Mental patients. Passports. Gun permits. Employees of the federal government. Lots of people."

Sharyn connected to the Internet as he spoke. She typed in "Rock Springs murder" and used the search engine. "So that could take a while?"

"*If* it's there." He put on his glasses and began to look at tests.

"Bingo! Becky Taylor, age nineteen, killed in Rock Springs, North Carolina."

"I remember it vaguely. She was knifed too?"

"Yes. Weapon not recovered. Police are baffled. No suspects."

"Sleepy little town, expensive school, blah blah blah," he finished for her.

She smiled. "Yeah. Something like that. Hey, here's something else. Aunt Selma and I were talking about it today. Another girl was killed there back in 1965. Her name was Anne Johnson."

"How was she killed?"

"I can't tell. It's only on microfiche at the newspaper office."

"That's not too bad," Nick remarked. "Two murders in almost forty years."

"Maybe they were both dating Tim Stryker!"

"I think you're getting jaded on this."

"Sorry." She zeroed in on Becky Taylor. "Her parents came down from Chicago to get her body. She was a good student, well liked according to this. But where did they find her?"

"The chief probably had the state do the forensics," he suggested. "You could ask for a copy."

"Good idea." She wrote down the info she needed. "That should tell me everything."

"These tests tell me that I must be a bad teacher."

"Why?"

"Because a lot of these kids can't tell a kidney from a small intestine."

"They do a look a lot alike," she answered.

He sighed and put the tests away. "Megan and Keith told me that they're engaged."

"They're getting married?"

"Apparently. That's what being engaged leads to. But not before they get out of school." He looked at her. "Think Kristie will be upset?"

"No. That's finished. I'm glad he's moving on too. I was dreading coming to a crime scene while he was recovering from their breakup."

Nick laughed and shook his head. "You are definitely wasted as a sheriff if the only thing you dread about a crime scene is a whiny college kid! You need to be a pathologist."

"Thanks but I just won the election. I'll stay where I am. And that wasn't what I meant."

"I know. I'm ready to go. How about a movie? Or do you have plans with Jack in an alley somewhere tonight?"

"Thanks but I'm washing my hair."

He raised one black brow skeptically.

"No, really. We only have a small water heater and I have

to plan around my mom using up the hot water. She's out tonight with Caison."

"I'm crushed but I understand. Still thinking about getting your own place?"

She nodded. "I might stay at the apartment after Mom moves back to the house. It wouldn't be bad for me. I haven't told her yet. She's not happy about the idea of me living on my own. She thinks I should live at home until I get married."

He reached across the corner of the desk and took her hand. "That might be possible."

Sharyn looked into his dark eyes and smiled. "Maybe. Someday. Right now, I have to get through being Ernie's best man. What do you know about giving a bachelor party?"

Jefferson Two Rivers called first thing in the morning. "I'm standing outside the courtroom, Sharyn, but I wanted to tell you that I went to see Sam yesterday."

"Did he talk to you?" she asked as she drove towards Rock Springs.

"A little. Most of it doesn't make any sense. He saw some people. They were attacking the girl. He tried to stop them. Someone dropped the knife. He picked it up without thinking. Then he tried to help the girl. The doctors up here seem to think he was hit pretty hard on the head. He has a concussion. That's why he's so mixed up. They're transferring him today to the local hospital. I'm coming down later to have a word with the police chief there. I know Sam can be difficult but I think they used extreme force to subdue him."

Sharyn thought through everything he said. "Sam said there was more than one assailant?"

"Yeah. Look, I have to go. I met the lawyer your aunt got for Sam. She seems pretty tough. I still hope he won't need her."

"I'll do what I can, Jeff."

"Thanks, Sharyn."

She closed her cell phone thoughtfully. So they might be

looking for more than one attacker. That was interesting. *If* Sam's judgment could be trusted.

Aunt Selma called Sharyn as she was leaving for the hospital that morning to visit Joe. She asked her to come out to the college again. Sharyn was planning on going there anyway since the state ME would be there looking things over. She wanted to hear his findings firsthand . . . unless Chief Murray objected.

Joe was restless and still angry that he had to be treated for rabies. Sharyn promised him that she was going to take care of the situation.

"Maybe if I didn't have to catch crazy critters," he conceded, "I might be willing to come back."

He looked so pale and strange sitting in the hospital bed without his sunglasses, that she hugged him. "Just get better, huh? I need you back at the office."

He smiled at her. "Was that to prove to Trudy that you're sensitive?"

"No. That was to prove to myself that you're going to be okay. I hate seeing you without your sunglasses. You just don't look right."

"I know. I'm going home today after the first injection. I'll be fine."

Joe, Ernie, and Ed were a part of her life for as long as she could recall. They came to family picnics and helped her down out of trees when she climbed too high. They were there when her father was killed even though Ed and Joe weren't sure about her being the sheriff in his place. She couldn't imagine a life without them.

Nick worked with her father too but he came later, as she was graduating from high school. She never thought they would be able to work together without fighting much less dating. But maybe the spark was always there. Maybe it just took some time to become a blaze.

She smiled as she pulled into the parking lot at the college. It was becoming familiar sharing her day with him. She liked it. She supposed she could imagine sharing more than that with him. Not right away. It was all too new. And she was having a good time the way they were.

"Sheriff Howard." Chief Murray greeted her as she climbed own out of the Jeep. "I thought you might be here today. The ME is already here. He's looking at the knife. Would you like to join us?"

"If you don't mind?"

"Not at all! Come on inside."

Officer Kaiser didn't look too pleased to see her. He barely nodded his head then looked away. Sharyn ignored him as the chief introduced her to the ME, Bobby Fisher.

"Nice to meet you, Sheriff Howard," Fisher said with an impish grin. He was a tiny man with a cropped head of sandy colored hair and the face of an elf. "I know your ME pretty well. Nick and I get together for a drink once in awhile."

"Nice to meet you too, sir."

"Please call me Bobby. Everybody does."

"Okay, Bobby." She shook his hand. "I'm Sharyn."

"Well, Sharyn." He cracked his knuckles. "Let's get the show on the road!"

He pulled on gloves and an apron then took the knife out of the plastic bag. He saved some of the blood in a container and sealed it. He marked it with the date and the case number. "I'll get back to you after I have a chance to type it and so forth."

Chief Murray nodded.

"Let's take a look at this now. Hopefully, there'll be some prints."

"I took it out of Two River's hand myself," Pike told him. "He wasn't wearing any gloves either. There's bound to be prints."

Bobby put on a jeweler's eye loupe and examined the knife under a bright light at the chief's desk. "This is interesting. It looks old. I'm not an expert but I'm betting this is at least a hundred-years-old. Maybe more. And definitely Cherokee glyphs on the handle. And a name of sorts here. Do you have someone else coming to look at it?"

"Yes. A professor from UNC is coming later. He specializes in this stuff."

"Good. The curve of the knife is a giveaway. I examined the girl this morning. The entry wounds definitely match this blade. There was no skin under her fingernails though. I don't think she had a chance to fight back."

"How's she doing?" Sharyn wondered.

Bobby looked at her with the loupe still in his eye. "You didn't hear? She died last night about ten. Too much trauma to her heart and lungs. She was bleeding from the spleen but they couldn't operate again since they couldn't stabilize her."

"I didn't know."

Chief Murray shook his head. "Sorry, Sharyn. I was on the phone with her parents all morning. Couldn't call you. They're coming in later today to get her. Terrible loss."

"There're prints all over. Let's get some tape and lift them off." Bobby saved them as he spoke. "We'll have to compare them but—"

"We have his prints right here." Howell offered Sam's prints saved on a slide to the ME.

Bobby took out his portable microscope. He examined the prints then lifted his head. "Sheriff?"

Sharyn looked through the eyepiece. The prints were the same. Her heart sank even though she knew they would probably be there.

"I don't see any other prints," Bobby said when he returned to the table. "Good job, Chief. You too, Officer. It's hard not to contaminate evidence in circumstances like this."

Both pieces of news made everything so much worse. Sharyn felt a little blindsided by it. Bobby was moving on in his examination of the evidence. She put the information from her mind and walked across the street with them.

Bobby Fisher was as energetic on the case as Nick was laconic. He darted from one side of the scene to the other as he snapped photos and muttered to himself. "This crime scene is useless."

"Why? It's where we found them," Pike defended.

"It's been exposed to the elements. There's dozens of different footprints here. Your students have been walking through here. The rain has washed everything away. I don't know how you expect me to tell anything like this!"

"Sorry," Howell muttered. "We did the best we could."

Bobby snapped off his latex gloves. "Never mind. What about the inside crime scene you mentioned?"

They took him into Lynette's dorm room. He looked the place over carefully, spraying some areas with Luminol but coming up with nothing. "I don't think anything happened here."

"What about the mess?" Pike asked, his voice starting to sound a little tense.

"She's a college girl! My daughter's dorm room looks the same way. What did you expect it to look like?"

Sharyn turned her head away to hide her smile.

"We thought all of this showed signs of a struggle," Howell added.

"Nothing is torn, despite the mess," Bobby pointed out. "No sign of blood. There was no trace of chemicals in her system or we could think she was subdued in some way. This way, we don't even have any evidence that she was taken from this room. Maybe she walked out the door and met the man outside. You did say it was after curfew?"

Pike glanced at his father-in-law. "Yeah, that's what we said."

Bobby shrugged. "There was no sign of sexual activity on her body. But maybe they didn't make it that far. Maybe she sneaked outside to meet him and they argued, then the suspect attacked her and wanted to kill her but you stopped him. That's probably what happened."

"Except you don't have any evidence to support any of that except finding Sam with her outside," Sharyn said. "Everything else is speculation."

"That may be," Bobby told her, stripping off his gloves again. "But the girl is dead. The chief and his men found the man with her outside. If the blood on the knife is hers and his prints are on it, I'd say it's a done deal."

"What about motive?" Sharyn asked again despite the last reception she got when she asked the question. "Did they even know each other? Did anyone see them together at any time?"

"All of that is up to the lawyers," Pike told her. "We did our job. They have to do theirs."

Howell agreed. "I'm afraid he's right, Sharyn. Your friend killed that girl. He's gonna be charged with murder."

When they were done speculating on what happened, Sharyn left them and started walking towards her aunt's office.

Pike followed her. "Where you going in such a big rush, Sheriff Howard?"

"I'm going to see my aunt." She stopped walking and waited for him.

"I hear your aunt's been asking around about Lynette Ashe. You have her doing your busy work for you?"

Sharyn was starting to dislike Pike Kaiser. "You're so busy making up scenarios that make Sam the killer, I thought it might be nice if we had a few ounces of the truth."

His eyes narrowed on her face. "You're causing trouble here that's not called for. Sheriff or not, I can ask you to leave Rock Springs."

She didn't back down. "You can *ask*. But I'm not doing anything illegal looking around."

"Wearing that uniform and snooping around the college is undermining my authority. And school grounds are private property." He nodded at her and put his hands on his waist. "I think you get my drift."

"I'm going to see my aunt, Officer. If you want to arrest me, go ahead."

When she reached her aunt's door, Sharyn glanced back. Pike was still watching her from beside the old magnolia tree. The icy wind blew the glossy deep green leaves. He stared at her for another minute then pushed past the tree and walked back towards the police station.

Taking a deep breath, she opened the door and went inside.

Aunt Selma was engrossed in conversation with Professor Neal. They looked up when she came in. "Sharyn, we may have discovered something important."

Sharyn sat down in a hard wooden chair. "Okay."

"Professor Neal has been gracious enough to offer his help. Since he was one of Lynette's teachers, we've been talking about her friends and her habits. But I think we may have found something even more important."

Sharyn waited while the two glanced at each other like conspirators in a plot.

"I think we know where the murder weapon came from." Aunt Selma's fierce blue eyes locked on her niece as she passed a photo to her.

"The day of the murder, a curio cabinet in my office was broken into," Professor Neal told her. "I reported it to Officer Kaiser. He came and took photos of it but that's all that was ever said about it. But if you'll look closely at that insurance photo, you'll see that it was a knife that was stolen. A ceremonial Cherokee knife. Now I haven't seen the knife that killed Miss Ashe but I have read a description of it in the papers and I was thinking the two could be the same."

Sharyn looked at the photo. "It's the same knife. You said you reported the break-in to Officer Kaiser?"

"Yes. He came over and took some pictures. He said he'd do what he could."

"Did you show him this photo?"

"Yes." Professor Neal paused. "You'd think he'd recognize it too if it's the same."

"You'd think. Can we take a look at your curio cabinet?" Sharyn asked.

"Of course! Right this way."

She stepped outside to get her fingerprint kit from her Jeep. She glanced towards the police station but there was no sign of the chief or his assistant. It was odd Pike didn't mention that the knife was stolen earlier from the professor. But that would make the investigation take a swing away from Sam. Unless they could prove that Sam stole the knife.

The professor's office was bigger and more lived in than Aunt Selma's. A huge gray slate fireplace flanked one wall. Two big leather chairs were set in corners close to it. His wide window overlooked the back of the campus and the planetarium building. The wood floors creaked under his wheelchair as he rolled into the room before Selma and Sharyn.

"Of course, I collect historical artifacts," he was telling them. "They come my way from time to time."

"How long have you had the knife?" Sharyn asked, glancing around the big, comfortable room.

"Only a few years. Here it is." He showed them the cabinet. "It's a hundred-years-old. I bought it at an auction on eBay."

The curio cabinet was six-feet tall and about four-feet wide with a handsome oak finish and beveled glass. The glass was still broken where the knife was stolen. Tiny shards of it covered the interior of the shelf. Clearly it was smashed in from the outside.

"If I may?" Sharyn took out her print kit.

"Oh please!" the professor enthused. "This is fascinating. Would you like some tea?"

Sharyn accepted and he went to his hotplate in the corner. She crouched down beside the cabinet and put on her gloves.

"Are you looking for fingerprints?" Aunt Selma queried softly, looking over her shoulder.

"Yep. It would seem like there wouldn't be any but sometimes, a person accidentally touches something when they pick up an object. Or they rest their hand on the outside without thinking."

The professor came back to join them while the tea brewed on the hotplate. The orange spice smell filled the room like the silence as they all watched for a fingerprint to appear.

Sharyn carefully brushed the glass shards out of the way. "Mind if I keep these?"

"No. Go ahead." The professor grinned at her. "This is exciting!"

Carefully, she used her brush to put the glass into an envelope for Nick to examine. She didn't dare give it to the chief and especially not Pike. Besides, if Bobby Fisher was gone, when would they get someone else to look at it?

"I don't see any prints," Aunt Selma told her as she watched Sharyn work.

"I don't either." Sharyn sighed. "Whoever did this was probably wearing gloves."

"Criminals are so smart these days." Selma sighed with her.

Sharyn took off her gloves and put away her print kit. There had to be more than one way to tackle the break-in since it was obviously tied to the murder. "Who knew about this collection, professor?"

"Well, probably everyone at the school." He handed her a cup of tea in a bright yellow mug with the school logo on it. "It's my pride and joy."

He went on to point out his fossils and other historic artifacts.

"What about this?" Sharyn asked pointing to a brown leather covered book.

"That's just an old diary. But look here. I have a gold doubloon believed to be part of Blackbeard's treasure. There's also a piece of wood from the hull of the ironclad Monitor. Picked it up myself three years ago." He scratched his white beard. "Now that was an adventure!"

Sharyn sipped her tea. "Do you keep your office door locked?"

"No. No one here does that."

"The chief told me there wasn't much crime."

"That's right. It's very quiet here. Usually." He glanced at Selma.

"That's true. I never thought to be afraid to walk the campus at night by myself."

"Except that there was another murder here five years ago," Sharyn pointed out. "The girl's name was Becky Taylor. Good student. No trouble."

"I've only been coming here to teach this class for the last two years," Selma replied. "And I didn't know the girl who was killed here in 1965."

Professor Neal shrugged. "Alas. If Becky Taylor was my student, I don't remember her. I remember the crime, of course. And the murder in '65. That one is a little more of a blur for me. I lost the use of my legs in a car accident at around the same time."

Sharyn focused in on the more recent crime. "So anyone could have come in here and stolen the knife."

"I'm afraid so. Even Lynette herself, I suppose. She did a lot of extra work for me. Lovely girl."

"She was in here often?"

"Yes quite a bit. She graded papers for me, did some side projects." The professor looked at her. "Good grief! Does that make me a suspect?"

Selma smiled and patted his gnarled hand. "I don't think so, Aaron. Sharyn is simply looking for an alternate way to explain the girl's death."

"But if Mr. Two Rivers didn't kill the girl, who did?"

"That's what we have to find out, sir." Sharyn got to her feet and put down the empty mug. "Thanks for the tea. I have to get back to Diamond Springs. If I find out anything else, I'll let you know."

"And we'll keep asking around," Selma promised with a wink at the professor.

"I'd like a chance to talk to some of her friends, Aunt Selma," Sharyn told her. "If you could arrange a meeting?"

"I could do that."

"What about me?" the professor asked eagerly. "What can I do?"

"Do you know what the inscription says on that knife?"

"No, but I may be able to find out. I have a friend who reads Cherokee glyphs."

"Great. Keep me posted."

"Thank you, Sheriff!"

Sharyn didn't usually get thanked for handing out assignments. She hugged her aunt goodbye and shook hands with the professor. "I'll get back with you as soon as I can. Call me if you need anything. And don't get in trouble."

Chief Murray was waiting at her Jeep as she was getting ready to leave. "Pike tells me we have a problem, Sharyn."

"I don't think so," she said as she stuffed her print kit and the envelope that held the glass shards into her jacket pockets.

"He tells me that you're investigating on your own over here." Howell smiled at her. "That doesn't sound like a co-operative effort between our departments. You are out of your jurisdiction here."

Sharyn leaned up against the Jeep's dirty red fender. "Chief, Sam Two Rivers didn't kill that girl. Your evidence is circumstantial and I don't think it'll hold up in court. In the meantime, the real killer is free to leave. If he or she hasn't already."

Chief Murray rubbed his ear and set his dark hat back on his head. "Sheriff, finding a man who's incoherent holding a bloody knife over a mutilated girl *isn't* circumstantial. You only think it is because he's your friend. But it's no skin off my nose if you want to keep looking for another killer."

"Thanks."

"I'll try to keep Pike from getting too territorial. He takes this kind of thing real personal, you know?"

"I understand. I appreciate you letting me look around."

"No problem."

Sharyn felt like they were through. She climbed up on her seat and put on her seatbelt.

Chief Murray tapped on the window and she rolled it down. "There's just one more thing you should probably know since you're determined to look into this closer."

"Yes?"

"We had the two cases analyzed, Lynette Ashe and that other girl, Becky Taylor."

Sharyn knew he was about to drop a bomb on her. She could feel it coming but there was nowhere to hide.

"Turns out that Becky Taylor worked with Mr. Two Rivers on an animal rescue program a week before she was killed. They're taking a look now at the knife wounds, matching them up and everything. Looks like we might get a twofer."

"Twofer?"

He grinned like a possum caught in a trashcan. "Two for the price of one. I think Mr. Sam Two Rivers killed both of those girls. Have a nice day, Sheriff."

Chapter Six

"**S**am will be released from the hospital tomorrow morning," Jefferson Two Rivers told Sharyn over coffee that evening. "He'll be taken to the Union County jail from there. Then he'll be arraigned on both counts of murder."

"I could bite my tongue off!" Sharyn exploded.

"You did the best you could for him."

"I gave the chief the idea that the two attacks could be related. Before I said something, it didn't occur to him."

He shrugged his broad shoulders. "Believe me, it was bound to come up. They were looking for someone to hang. Sam was a convenient target."

"Can he speak now? Will he be all right?"

"He's fine. That police chief and his officer are going to be up on charges of abusing his rights before I get done with them. They're lucky they didn't kill him! I'd like to bring down some of my boys and show them what it's like."

"But that won't help Sam," she reminded him calmly.

"No. It won't."

They sat together at the diner down the block from the sheriff's office in Diamond Springs. The night was turning cold. There was frost on the plate glass window beside them. Outside on the street, traffic was light. A pale crescent moon sailed over the top of Diamond Mountain, reflected in the still blackness of Diamond Lake in the center of town.

"The one thing that shouldn't match up is the knife," Sharyn told him. "The murder weapon was stolen from a professor's cabinet at the college. When they finish the tests, the murder weapon should be different."

"Which doesn't amount to much. What does that mean? He murdered them with two different knives. That's what I'd think if it were my case. He still looks guilty to me and I'm his brother."

"That's true, I suppose. With everything else against him, it's going to be hard to dig him out."

"Is this a private confab or can anyone join in?" Ernie asked, coming up to the table.

"Please, Deputy. I appreciate the help you've given my brother. Jefferson Two Rivers."

"Ernie Watkins." He shook the other man's hand. "I wish we could do more. Sam's a good fella."

"He has his problems," Jefferson acknowledged. "But I don't think he killed either one of those girls."

"Those problems didn't help him any," Ernie said, sitting beside Sharyn and ordering coffee. "I heard on the news that he's going to be arrested for both murders."

"That's right."

"Was he able to tell you anything about what happened?" Ernie asked him with a smile for the waitress as she brought his coffee.

"He told me that he heard a sound in the bushes as he was leaving the campus after spending some time with Selma Howard. Your aunt?" Jefferson glanced at Sharyn.

"Yes."

"Sam went to check on it because he thought he heard something that sounded like a muffled cry. He probably thought it was an animal. You know Sam. He saw several people run away into the darkness behind the dorm house. He found the girl and tried to help her. I think he picked up the knife and looked at it without thinking about it."

"That's pure instinct," Sharyn remarked. "But what was he saying about an evil spirit when we saw him?"

"I'm not sure," Jefferson admitted. "The word you told me

is Cherokee for evil spirit. I asked him about it. He didn't know what I was talking about. He can't recall seeing you at the jail. The doctor thinks it was the concussion. Sam didn't know what he was saying, babbling out of his mind."

"Sheriff told me they cracked his skull," Ernie added. "I hope you plan on filing charges?"

"I already have. They say he resisted arrest. Sam said they came down on him when they saw him. He didn't even have a chance to get to his feet. Case in point. One of his fingers was broken when he held out his hand to protect himself. Doctor is willing to testify that he's covered with defensive wounds."

Ernie shook his head as he sipped his coffee. "I can't say I'm never tempted."

"I can't either," Jefferson agreed. "But it was bad to see Sam laid out that way. It made me remember why I'm tempted but I don't smash suspects in the head."

Sharyn went back to the Cherokee word Sam uttered when they saw him. "So you're sure the evil spirit word didn't mean anything?"

"Not as far as I can tell. I'm hoping to see the knife for myself. The evidence against Sam says it's a Cherokee artifact. Makes it sound like he was on the warpath or something. The jury will eat it up."

"The collector at the college has a picture of it for his insurance," Sharyn told him. "I could get him to fax me a copy and send it to you. I don't like the racial overtones either but I think the knife could be important to the case."

"Please. I don't know if it matters but I'd like to see it. Sam can't recall even seeing the knife. Just the girl lying on the ground." Jefferson glanced at his watch. "I have to go. It's a long trip back home but I wanted to stop and talk with you, Sharyn. Plus I needed to chill after talking to those two morons in Rock Springs!"

"I'm glad you did." She took his hand as he stood up to go. "I'll get that picture to you. Let me know if there's anything else I can do."

"You've done so much, I don't know where to start to thank you. Sam's chosen to isolate himself from his family in Cherokee. But I'm glad he has people like you down here to depend on. If you need anything, let me know."

"Thanks. Have a safe trip back."

Ernie glanced at Sharyn when they were alone. "I didn't want to say anything in front of Sam's brother. But I found some interesting similarities about the two murders that are bound to come out if they try to play this as some kind of serial killing. It's not good."

She took out her notebook. "You know, normally I'd be rooting for you to find this stuff."

"Normally," he agreed, "we're trying to convict someone. First student, Rebeccah Taylor. She was nineteen. Blond hair, blue eyes, about five-foot-five, from Chicago. She was stabbed to death. They found her on the stairs of the Piper mansion five years ago. On January nineteenth."

"The main office." She looked up at him. "The dates were that close?"

"Yep. Lynette Ashe. Twenty-one. Blond hair, blue eyes. Five-foot-six, from Ohio. She was stabbed to death just outside one of the dorms. On January tenth."

"And we already know there was a direct link between Sam and Becky Taylor." She closed her notebook. "Did anything jump out at you about a relationship between Sam and Lynette?"

"Nope. But they lucked out on finding that about Becky. There was a website with photos from the animal rescue camp that year. Sam and her were in the same photo."

"So as far as we know, Lynette didn't help Sam with any animal rescues?"

"I talked with Bruce Bellows earlier. There was no animal camp last year because of the dry conditions in the mountains. Last year was Lynette's first semester at Piper. But I get a sneaky suspicion that Chief Murray is holding another card up his sleeve on this."

"Yeah, Just waiting to pop it out at me, huh?"

"Where do you want to go from here?" Ernie finished his coffee and sat back.

"I don't know." Sharyn realized what time it was. "Is it eight-thirty? Shouldn't you be home with Annie?"

"Maybe."

"Maybe?"

He shrugged. "I want to help you with this case. I know you can't work on it much during office hours. And from the look of things, you can use all the help you can get."

"Is there a problem with you and Annie?"

"I don't know."

"Ernie! As your best man, I think you should talk to me."

"Sharyn—" he started, then collapsed into silence.

"More coffee, Deputy?"

"No, thanks, Betty Jean."

"What is it?" Sharyn demanded in a low, worried voice.

He smiled at her and adjusted his glasses. "I think it's called cold feet. I've been alone for a long time. Maybe I'm not ready to sell my house and move in with her. Maybe we should wait for a while."

"You love her, Ernie. You've loved her since you were sixteen."

"You don't need to remind me of that. I know."

"And she loves you," Sharyn continued. "Annie is the right person for you."

He leaned forward, his gray eyes focused on her. "Don't you think I've said all of this to myself a million times?"

She leaned forward until their faces were inches apart. "Then what's the problem?"

"Fear. Cold, hard fear." He swallowed hard then continued. "The kind of fear that knots up in your belly and clamps down on your chest until you can't breathe. It's worse than anytime I looked down the barrel of somebody else's gun. Worse than when I was fighting in Vietnam. I've never been so scared in my whole life."

"Ernie!" She squeezed his hand. "You only have to think about Annie. If you think about Annie and how much you love her, you can do it. Think about how you felt when you were afraid you were going to lose her at the training school that night. Think about how you felt the day she told you that she loved you."

He put his hand to her face. His eyes were misty. "How did you get so smart?"

Sharyn smiled. "I had good teachers." Her cell phone rang. "Sheriff Howard."

"You know," Nick, drawled at the other end, "I didn't mind so much being jilted for a senator. Even if it *was* Jack Winter. But Ernie? He's only a deputy. He doesn't even make as much money as I do."

She laughed. "Where are you?"

"Outside the window watching your romantic tableau. I thought you were washing your hair?"

"Get in here!"

"I would but you know what they say about three being a crowd."

"Who is it?" Ernie asked, glancing around.

"It's Nick." She closed her cell phone. "He's worried that I'm dating you too."

"You mean as well as the good senator?" He grinned his lopsided grin. "My how you do get around, Sheriff Howard!"

"Yeah. That's me. Good time, party girl!"

The three of them ended up eating grilled cheese sandwiches and greasy french fries at the diner for dinner. Sharyn told them about her encounter with Officer Kaiser that day.

Ernie stuck a fry in ketchup. "You better be careful. That man sounds like trouble. Look what he did to Sam."

"What did he do?" Nick asked.

"Sam had a concussion and a broken finger from the police beating him when they found him with Lynette Ashe," Sharyn explained. "His brother says he didn't even have a chance to stand up much less fight back."

"So that's why he was incoherent."

"And that's why you shouldn't feel like they wouldn't do

it to you if you get in their way," Ernie cautioned Sharyn again.

"We're on to something, Ernie. I can't let this go yet."

"Let Selma do the leg work," he answered. "Sam's her man anyway."

She laughed. "Yeah. How weird is that?"

"Don't ask me. I'm getting married pretty soon here. Speaking of which, when is the bachelor party?"

"Saturday night," Nick replied as Sharyn's phone rang and she answered it. "About nine. At Stag Inn Doe."

"Duke's old place?" Ernie asked in surprise, hearing the name of the infamous nightclub. "That place has been busted so many times, they can't keep the doors locked at night anymore!"

Nick waggled his eyebrows. "Yeah. That's the idea."

They waited while Sharyn spoke quietly. She closed the phone and looked at them. "There's been another robbery. They didn't scope this one out as well. JP says the wife is away but the husband came home and found them there."

"He's alive?" Ernie was already on his feet. "A witness?"

"Looks like it."

"I'll ride with you two," Nick said, taking out his cell phone. "It will save me from having to get my SUV from the hospital."

They took Sharyn's Jeep out to the same area as the last six break-ins. The paramedics were already at the scene, treating the surprised husband. Megan and Keith rolled up in the forensics van at the same time.

"Sheriff Howard!" JP greeted her. "We got lucky. The man is not seriously hurt. I was on patrol about five minutes away when I got the call."

"Good job, JP," she commended him. "We'll take it from here so you can finish your patrol."

"Yes, ma'am!"

Sharyn was surprised when she approached the paramedic van and found county building inspector John Schmidt sitting inside. "John! I didn't know you lived out here!"

He smiled and winced. "Actually, I don't yet. Not until tomorrow. My wife and I are moving in across the street. That's why I was out here, checking to make sure everything was set up. This house belongs to my son and his wife. They're at Disney World with their kids this week."

Sharyn glanced at Ernie. It might be the break they were looking for. "Did you see anything?"

"I saw the van. That's why I came over. I knew Mike wasn't here. It was kind of late to be contractors anyway. I'm sorry. I didn't really see anything. I walked up behind the van. Someone hit me in the back of the head. Lucky for me, I have a hard head. If I wouldn't have rolled out of the way, I guess they would've backed right over me. I heard voices and saw feet running out of the house. There was a group of them. Just like it said in the paper."

"Is he okay?" Ernie asked the paramedic.

"He should go in and have some tests to be sure but he's probably okay. Just a bad bump."

"You were lucky," Ernie agreed. "Mind if we take a look inside the house?"

"Go ahead. Whatever it takes to get these people out of there! Mary Jo is worried silly about moving out here tomorrow."

Sharyn nodded and Ernie left them alone. "John, I understand how your wife feels. I've been looking for a house out here that we can use to trap the group of burglars."

The burly ex-contractor looked at her. "What do I have to do?"

Sharyn sat in her office early the next morning looking at photos of the seven houses that were hit by the gang. David and JP were leaving for home. Marvella, Cari, and Ernie were walking in the back door.

"You're here early," Ernie said when he saw her there.

"I have that five-minute meeting with the commission about animal control today. I wouldn't want to be late."

"What are you looking at?" He walked around the desk to look over her shoulder.

"Pictures of the outside of the houses that were broken into. Somehow these people know when a house is empty. How did they know Mike Schmidt was going to be out of town with his family?"

"I don't know, Sheriff. Are you looking for little signs posted in the front yard?"

"Maybe that's it." She sat up and blinked her eyes, suddenly wide awake. "Maybe there are little signs in the front yard."

"I was only fooling, Sheriff, I—"

"Look, Ernie! The one thing all the houses have in common. They all get the Gazette delivered. What's the first thing we always tell people so that burglars won't know their house is empty when they're gone?"

"Stop delivery." He nodded and stroked his mustache as he looked at the newspaper boxes on each picture. "It's possible, I guess. But there's a lot of those paper boxes around there."

Sharyn sobered immediately. "Someone who works at the circulation department at the Gazette could be tipping the gang. Do you think we could get an employee list without alerting anyone?"

"Yeah, sure. We can ask for a total employee list broken down into departments."

"We still can't walk in and pick them up. We won't get anywhere like that. But we can test the theory by having John call and tell them when he wants his new circulation to start. He can make sure to tell them that he and Mary Jo will be on vacation."

"That could work."

"Let's give it a try. I'll have John call it in before he leaves this morning. Do we have surveillance set up inside the house?"

He yawned. "As of midnight last night."

"I want someone there all the time. Marvella would be perfect for the first shift. Have her use her car and we'll reimburse her. John leaves at noon. Let's make sure we get them. This may be our last chance. You never know when they're going to decide to move on to somewhere else."

"I'm on it."

Sharyn put on her hat. "I'm going to talk to the commission."

The newly elected commission for Diamond Springs and Montgomery County was a whole other beast. There were muffins on the tables in pretty baskets and coffee at the door. Brightly colored flowers graced the dais. Julia Richmond was in her element, shaking hands and smiling at the other commissioners while reporters took their pictures.

"Guess I better watch my step," Todd Vance, the newly re-elected mayor muttered to Sharyn as she sat beside him. "The next election, she could want *my* job."

Sharyn smiled. "A muffin in every voting booth?"

"Exactly. You're not worried because you know she doesn't want *your* job, Sheriff! Only Roy was crazy enough for that and look where it got him!"

The commission finally called itself to order. Sharyn was first on the agenda to speak. The secretary reminded her that she had only five minutes before they moved on to more pressing issues.

"Madame Chairperson," Sharyn addressed the commissioners from the new speaker's platform. "My deputies are being hampered from performing their duties by the added burden of animal control. Right now, one of my officers, untrained in handling or containing wild animals, is having rabies shots because he was bitten by a rabid raccoon. He's a good deputy, but none of us have the specialized knowledge that it takes for this occupation. We're defenders of the law. Not wildlife managers. I ask that you reconsider your decision to do away with animal control and reinstate it as a separate county entity. Thank you."

Sharyn took her seat. She said what she came to say. Now she had to wait for the commission to move on to the next speaker before she could escape.

"If there are no questions," the secretary began to move forward.

"I have a question." Julia Richmond, the richest woman in Montgomery County pressed forward.

The secretary looked completely bemused by the response. "O-of course, Mrs. Richmond."

"Sheriff Howard, what would it cost to reinstate animal control?"

Sharyn glanced around the room, not expecting anything more than a terse statement that they would take it under advisement. "I have no idea, ma'am."

"You came before us with no facts or figures?"

"I didn't expect to set up the plan, ma'am."

Julia frowned. "Does anyone know?"

Bruce Bellows shot to his feet and waved his hand like a schoolboy. "I do, ma'am. I have a plan worked out already. As you know, county wildlife management took care of animal control during the drought and while we had a problem with the fires last fall. When I heard that the sheriff meant to ask about it, I put some things together."

Mayor Vance moaned softly. "We'll be here all day!"

Sharyn ignored him, amazed by Bruce's willingness to consolidate wildlife management and control permanently. She looked over his proposal even as the commission looked at it.

"Well, I've seen enough." Julia Richmond picked up her antiqued white gavel. "I think we should vote on it."

"All of the commission isn't here, Madame Chairperson," Ty Swindoll said, covering his microphone uselessly.

"Well then they'll have to be here from now on, won't they? Maybe it would be good for them to have a reason to be here!"

Betty Fontana sipped at her water, clearly bemused by the entire proceeding.

"All in favor raise their hand."

There was some mumbling in the group but most held up their hands in favor of it.

"All opposed?" Julia glared at the only one foolhardy enough to put up his hand. He quickly changed his vote. The gavel descended. "The motion is passed to recreate the animal control unit. It will be headed by county wildlife manager Bruce Bellows."

Sharyn was speechless. Bruce gave out a loud whoop and hugged the commission secretary.

Todd Vance shifted in his seat. "Gonna be a fun term, eh, sheriff?"

"This begins to pave the way for what I believe is going to be one of our most important pieces of legislation," Julia continued, "the separation of the county and city law enforcement."

Sharyn couldn't stop herself. She stood up. "Ma'am?"

Julia smiled benevolently. "You heard me, Sheriff. Diamond Springs needs its own police force. The sheriff's department would still have jurisdiction over felonies and would maintain its office in the city. But the local police would handle things like robberies, traffic accidents and minor offenses. Diamond Springs is growing. So is the county that surrounds us. We have to consider what the next step should be in quality law enforcement."

"You can't speak anymore," the commission secretary hissed at Sharyn. She cleared her throat and got to her feet. "The commission will hear the next request to ban potbelly pigs within the city limits of Diamond Springs."

Sharyn walked out of the courthouse and put on her hat. Things were changing all right. The rumors were true. The plan wasn't complete yet but the sheriff's office was going to be joined by a police department in Diamond Springs.

She took Trudy and Ernie into her office and explained the situation. "It's not a done deal yet but it's coming. I'd like some kind of note sent out to everyone, including the volunteer deputies. I don't want anyone to see this in the newspaper without having some idea first."

Trudy finished writing in her memo pad. "I'll get right on it. You say they're going to keep the sheriff's office here?"

"I don't know about that yet. We may stay here and the

police department may have another office in the courthouse. We'll have to see."

"I'll take care of it, Sheriff."

Ed joined them as he came in from patrol. He grinned at Trudy as she passed him and she stumbled over the trashcan. "What's up?" Sharyn explained the situation. "Good! Joe will be happy to hear no more chasing around after those animals!"

"I'm too old for this," Ernie whined. "A police force in Diamond Springs? The sheriff's department handling the county?"

"It sounds like we'll handle everything but minor things that come up within the city. I don't know yet, Ernie. We'll have to wait and see what happens."

"Who's going to head the new police department?" Ed asked.

"I don't know that either. I suppose they'll appoint someone," Sharyn answered. "In the meantime, we have a gang of burglars to catch."

"Marvella is on her way over there now," Ernie said. "She'll take first watch. I sent Cari home for the day so she could take the next one."

"Sounds good."

"I'm going out on patrol with Ernie." Ed laughed. "That's taken us back a while, huh?"

"Yeah. Way back!"

"Cheer up. Joe should be back in two weeks and three days. Then you can spend all your time with the computer again!"

Sharyn laughed. "See you two later!"

"I took care of the newspaper angle while you were out," Ernie said as he was leaving. "We should be getting that list faxed to us sometime today."

"Thanks, Ernie." Sharyn poured herself a cup of coffee.

"Phone for you, Sheriff," Trudy yelled. "It's Nick."

"Thanks, Trudy." Sharyn ignored Ernie's anguished sigh as he left the office, and picked up the phone. "Hi Nick."

"Good morning! I heard you've been busy this morning."

"Yeah." She sat down behind her desk. "No more animal patrols."

"I know Joe will be glad to hear it."

"And they confirmed the rumor. They *are* going to create a police department for Diamond Springs."

"How will it work?"

"I don't know yet. I'm sure they'll tell me when they know."

Nick laughed. "Well, I have some news. I don't have any takers yet on that thumbprint. But I got the hair DNA back from Raleigh. Megan was right. It is from a woman. She was right about the dye too."

"Guess that means I'm out of a job in pathology."

"Megan knows her hair dye," he said with a smile in his voice. "I guess you shouldn't quit your day job. Strands match DNA from both break-ins but no one who lives in or visits the houses. The chances are that they come from a member of the gang."

"So we're dealing with at least one woman."

"That's what it looks like."

"What now?"

"We wait to have a head full of them to compare the strands to. Until then, it's pretty useless. We can learn a lot from DNA but not the person's name or where to find them. There was nothing at the house last night. I don't think they even had a chance to get inside."

"Okay. Thanks, Nick. What about the glass from that break-in at the college?"

"I haven't had a chance to go through it yet. I'll have to let you know."

"Sure. I didn't mean to sound like I was rushing you."

"Lunch?"

"Maybe. Call me closer to noon, huh?"

"I have everything set up for Ernie's party Saturday. There's this girl who dances with balloons--"

"Don't tell me," she cautioned with a frown, "let me be surprised."

"Okay. I'll talk to you later. I'm in class all morning if you need me."

"Thanks."

"Fax coming through for you from Professor Neal at Piper College," Trudy yelled.

"Gotta go," Sharyn said to Nick. "I'll talk to you later."

Professor Neal's fax was clear. But she wasn't sure if she could make out all the markings she saw on the knife when she examined it at the police station in Rock Springs. The six-inch curved blade made a powerful statement without the writing. She hoped Jefferson would be able to tell something about it.

"Trudy, fax this picture to this number." She gave Trudy the fax number of the Cherokee sheriff's department. "Thanks."

"No problem, Sheriff." Trudy shuddered when she looked at the picture of the knife. "Evil looking, isn't it?"

"I guess it should be since it killed a woman."

"Yeah. What are those markings on the handle?" Trudy pressed her nose close to the picture.

"That's what I hope to find out."

Sharyn sat back down in her office. A packet of information from the SBI office had arrived in the mail. It contained all of the information about Becky Taylor's death five years ago. The pictures were graphic. The girl was sprawled on the steps to the main office like a commercial photo shoot. Blood was everywhere. The ME's report was terse. The girl died from extensive organ damage inflicted by a blade about six inches long. Cuts showed a curved angle to the knife. No weapon was present on the scene.

She frowned. It sounded a lot like the same knife to her. It would to a jury too. She picked up the phone to call the professor for more information about when and where he collected the knife. There was no answer. She left him a voice mail and went back to work looking through the file.

She compared Lynette's file to Becky's. Chief Murray was

gracious enough to send it to her. He was very sure of his case against Sam. The two girls were very similar. Not only in appearance but also in academics and placement in the school. Both girls were well liked and well thought of by their teachers.

There was a slight change in Lynette Ashe's school history in the last few months. Her grades slipped. She was cited for bad attendance and smoking in the dorm room. She was caught being out after curfew. There was nothing like that in Becky's file. There was no record of anything unusual until she was found dead on the morning of January 19.

Were the dates significant? Both murders occurred in January. Sharyn searched but couldn't find anything that coincided with the two deaths. No school activities that were unusual. No dances or field trips. Nothing she could link the deaths to. Maybe it was after Christmas blahs. Both girls stayed at the school during the three weeks the place was shut down for the holidays. She made a note of it even though she couldn't imagine what difference it made.

Her phone rang, startling her away from the files on her desk.

"Sharyn? Howell Murray here. I just thought you should know that Mr. Two Rivers was arraigned in court a few minutes ago. He was charged with both counts of first-degree murder. Sounded pretty good today. He had plenty to say."

"Did he admit to the murders?"

"Nope, but I think we've got a pretty good case against him."

"Except motive," she reminded him again. "Sam had no reason to hurt those two girls."

Murray chuckled. "A man don't always need a motivation that other people understand, Sharyn. I *know* you know that! Sometimes, a man does things because he has to."

"Thanks for calling, Chief."

"Oh, there's one more little thing that might interest you."

Here it comes! "Yes?"

"Your aunt and Professor Neal tried to break in here early this morning. I think they were trying to tamper with the evidence before we send it on to the county for the trial. I've got them in custody over here. You might want to think about arranging some bail."

Chapter Seven

"**O**f all the crazy things to do." Sharyn blasted her aunt and the professor from behind the cell doors in Rock Springs' jail. "What were you thinking?"

"I wanted to be sure the knife was the same knife that was stolen from Professor Neal," Selma whispered. "It was my idea."

"But it was a valid one," the professor defended her. "Suppose it was different and we were searching for the wrong thing? It could throw the case off completely."

"This is great." Sharyn paced the cement floor. "Breaking and entering is a serious charge. The chief plans to add tampering with evidence. That's a felony. Those charges carry a lot of weight. You could both go to jail."

"I hardly think any jury would convict us!" the professor argued. "I've never even had so much as a parking ticket!"

"Speak for yourself." Sharyn glared at her aunt. "I had to arrest Aunt Selma for assault on a county surveyor last year!"

The professor looked at Selma. She shrugged her shoulders beneath her shawl. "He was trespassing on my land."

"Perhaps we should call our lawyers?" Professor Neal suggested.

"My lawyer is in court with Sam today," Selma told him. "That's why I called—"

There was a disturbance in the outside office. Sharyn heard the raised voices and shook her head. "You didn't!"

Selma nodded proudly. "I did what was necessary in this situation!"

"What's going on?" The professor tried to peer through the bars at the door.

The door to the holding cell area was thrown open. Faye Howard was dressed in her most expensive faux mink coat. She stood beside ex-senator Caison Talbot who was holding his cane towards the heavens, blustering about injustice and indecency.

"Simmer down, sir." Chief Murray hastened back to where he was holding his prisoners. "I didn't realize these people were relatives of yours. We'll have them free in no time."

"That's more like it!" Caison held his head high. The white lion's mane of hair that crowned his head surrounded his ruddy face like a halo. "I don't know what this world is coming to when good, decent folk can't take part in the due process of the law!"

Howell Murray's hands trembled as he released Selma and the professor from the cell. He glanced at Sharyn and shook his head. "You didn't tell me you were related to the senator!"

Sharyn couldn't answer that question without laughing out loud. She walked quickly out of the station and waited for the comedy to come to its end. Selma was right. She did what she had to do. She knew if she called her sister-in-law what Faye would do.

She could hear the senator continue to rant inside, even though he had what he came for. He was impressive. She had to give him that. There were many times she would rather have faced a criminal with a gun than the onslaught of his extensive vocabulary.

She looked at the college campus across the street. The sunlight pointed up its age and the almost rustic simplicity of its buildings. All of the buildings on that side of the street were part of the original campus that was created by Elwood Piper from his plantation. The new buildings were on the same side as the police station.

She watched as the girls ran from class to class across the

street. The wind blew their books and papers and tugged at their hair. She was surprised that the college didn't build an overhead walkway to protect them from traffic and the weather. Three hundred and fifty students ran back and forth across the street every day. Traffic wasn't too steady but the weather would be a problem any time of the year.

That two murders happened here, so similar and so close together, was astounding. That they could happen in this tiny community was bound to impress and horrify a jury. No one expected that kind of thing to go on in a place like Rock Springs. It was the picture perfect ad for a close-knit, secluded girls' college.

Sharyn shivered. She wouldn't send a daughter of hers to school here. She couldn't suppress that creepy feeling she always got when she was there.

Caison was finished with the chief and Officer Kaiser. He emerged with Faye's hand tucked into the crook of his arm. His long black wool coat was the perfect foil for her. Selma and the professor followed them outside. They all burst out laughing when they reached Caison's limousine.

"That was fun!" Faye proclaimed.

"I knew you'd come through!" Selma hugged her. She held out her hand to Caison. "Thanks."

"My pleasure! I almost forgot how good it feels to wield that power!"

Sharyn walked slowly to the side of the limo. "I hate to bring all of you down from this but it wasn't a party and I don't expect to see anything like this again!"

Selma frowned and Faye raised her chin a notch.

Caison wasn't cowed at all. "Young woman, you don't know what fun is!"

"Fun doesn't include getting arrested, sir. I thought *you'd* know that!"

Before Sharyn could protest, Caison took her arm and marched her up the sidewalk away from the limo. "I do know that, Miss! Don't be impertinent! I was helping your mother and your aunt. I thought *you'd* appreciate it!"

Sharyn studied his lined face. He definitely looked older and a little less intimidating since his heart attack and losing the election. But not much. "I do appreciate it, sir. Thank you. I just don't want it to happen again."

"I'm sure Selma thought she was doing the right thing. She was trying to save her fiancé."

Sharyn didn't think Selma and Sam's relationship went that far, but she didn't say so.

"And as far as my knowing about jail, look to yourself! I can't believe you don't have any better sense than to allow yourself to get worked up over Jack Winter! The man will strip your soul, Sharyn. Mark my words!"

"I appreciate you worrying about me, sir. But I'm not involved with Mr. Winter. The whole thing with the gift was a mix up. I'm not even sure he meant me to have it."

He waved his cane. "I'm too old and too tired for lies, Sharyn. We both know what he meant. Stay away from him. Watch your back!"

"Caison!" Faye waved her hand for him. "Are we going for brunch?"

"Yes, ma'am!" His blue gaze was direct and sharp on Sharyn's face. "Heed my words, young woman! You're smart. I'll give you that. But he's smarter!"

Sharyn stood on the sidewalk and let him walk away. Selma and the professor stayed behind. They hurried across the street to Selma's office. Sharyn joined them.

"I know it was wrong, Sharyn," Selma told her before she could say anything else. "It won't happen again. But we did find out that the knife is the same knife that was stolen from Professor Neal."

"Yes!" the professor chimed in.

Selma shed her shawl and started some coffee. "I heard they indicted Sam this morning. Was it on both charges?"

"Yes. I'm sorry. This isn't looking good for him. But I talked to his brother last night." Sharyn filled her in on the details of what Jefferson told her. "I sent a fax with a picture of the knife to him this morning. Maybe he'll be able to tell us something else about it."

"But you feel this knife was used in both killings?" The professor frowned, puzzled. "I can't believe I had such a thing in my possession."

"How could you know?" Sharyn asked him. "I'd like to know how you came to have it."

"Of course." The professor unwrapped his gray scarf from his neck. Selma helped him with his coat. "I go to auctions around the area. I bought the knife two years ago at an auction. I suppose I should tell the police."

"You should," Sharyn agreed. "It's not going to do us any good to keep it a secret. They pretty much have everything they need to convict Sam."

Selma shook her head. "So they'll say he broke in and took the knife to kill the girl?"

"There's one good thing about that. It makes it harder for them to say the knife was used in both murders. If the knife were still in his possession, the case would be easier. It might create some doubt in the minds of the jurors about him committing both murders."

"Or make it look like he was a serious serial killer." Professor Neal scratched his graying head. "I agree with the sheriff. It sounds bad for him."

"We lined up all of the girls who were friends with Lynette." Selma turned from the negative to the positive as she always did. "All of them are in her dorm as well. Would you like to talk to them?"

Sharyn considered it. "Could we work that out without confronting Chief Murray?"

Selma glanced at Professor Neal. "I believe we could. What do you think?"

He shrugged. "We could have all of them called down to a conference room. I could say I was questioning them about breaking into my cabinet. No one would have to know it was about the murder."

"That works," Sharyn agreed. "How long would it take?"

"Twenty minutes, maybe." Selma looked at her watch. "Let's do it!"

Three of the four young women summoned to the hasty meeting waited and whispered together on the sofa in the conference room. On the other side of the room, Selma, Professor Neal and Sharyn waited for the last girl to show. When she finally pushed open the door and peeked in, they were ready.

"Professor Howard, Professor Neal," the new woman began, "what's going on?"

"We'd like to ask you a few questions about your friend Lynette," Selma began, putting on her glasses so she could read from the cards Sharyn wrote. In case the chief found out, Sharyn decided she could plead that she was there but didn't ask the questions. It made her less active in the investigation. Hopefully, it made her less likely to tread on any official toes.

"Lynette?" Susan Atmore demanded. "I thought we were here to discuss a break-in at the professor's office?"

The other three girls joined her. Bonnie Moss, Robbie Faggart, and Joanne Sikes. It was easy for Sharyn to spot their leader. Susan stood at the apex of the group. She was the only one to question what was going on. The three others waited for her to speak.

Selma cleared her throat. "Well, Miss Atmore, we're going to discuss that as well. But we're concerned about your friend, Lynette, too. Did you know that her grades were dropping before she was killed?"

"No."

"I knew. We were all having problems this semester," Bonnie said, but was quelled with a look from Susan.

"Did something happen this semester?" Aunt Selma tried to pin the girl down.

"Nothing . . . unusual, exactly." Bonnie's voice trailed off.

"Did you know she was getting in trouble with the dean over poor attendance, smoking, and staying out after curfew?"

"Everybody gets in trouble with the dean at some time or

another," Susan told her. "Lynette smoked. We all smoke. We're old enough."

"What about Tim Stryker? How close was he to Lynette?"

"They dated for a while," Joanne answered. "Didn't they?"

"Yeah. They were tight."

"Until they broke up," Susan supplied. "He had a bad temper. We thought he killed poor Lynette until we hard about that other guy."

"Did Lynette know Mr. Two Rivers?" Selma queried.

Susan shrugged, her blond hair flipping over her shoulder. "I don't know. She was getting a ride to Diamond Springs to see Tim a few times a week. We had to pick her up there a few times when she couldn't get a ride back. Maybe Mr. Two Rivers was taking her there. We all knew he was coming here to see *you*, Professor Howard."

Selma blushed down to the roots of her copper-red hair but she continued. "Did any of you see Lynette go out that night? Do you know if she was meeting anyone?"

Susan stared at her. "We answered all of these questions for Chief Murray. Why don't you ask him?"

The interview went from bad to nothing quickly after that. Sharyn studied Susan Atmore from her long blond hair to her strong arms and booted feet. Her mind began collecting and sorting data, considering the possibilities. The other two girls were brunettes and Joanne had coal black hair. But Susan's long blond hair stuck in her mind.

Selma glanced at Sharyn who nodded back at her. "Well, I guess that's it. Thank you, girls."

"You didn't even ask us about Professor Neal's cabinet," Susan reminded her.

The professor nodded. "You're right, Susan. Do you have any idea who broke into my curio cabinet?"

Susan smiled. "Maybe you should ask Lynette since the two of you were *so* close. Oops! She's dead, isn't she? I have to get back to class."

Sharyn stood up and grabbed the door for her, letting Susan flounce past her as she left the room. She put out a hand and snagged a strand of Susan's golden blond hair with her ring. "Gotcha!"

Susan glanced back at her but didn't say anything. The other girls followed her quickly.

"Well?" Selma asked, emotionally exhausted by the ordeal. "Did we learn anything helpful?"

"I'll let you know," Sharyn promised. "Keep an eye on them for me. And Professor, go ahead and let the chief know that he has your knife. Why didn't you two tell him that when he caught you breaking into the office?"

Selma drew herself up proudly. "We didn't want to squeal!"

"Besides," the professor noted, "it didn't do me any good to report the theft when it happened. Why bother telling them again?"

Sharyn shook her head. "No more breaking and entering, please. See what you can find out about those four girls for me. Who they date, how their grades are, what they do in their spare time."

"We will." Selma bit her lip. "Do you think I could go and see Sam at the county jail?"

"Once they get him settled in today, you should be able to. I want to go and see him too. Maybe we could go together tomorrow?"

"All right. Thank you, Sharyn." Selma hugged her tightly. "I love you."

"I love you too. Don't worry. We'll think of something."

Sharyn avoided the police station and managed to get out of Rock Springs without a confrontation. She'd carefully put the single strand of blond hair into a plastic bag and sealed it.

Ernie called to say that Marvella was leaving her post and Cari was taking over for the next shift. There was no sign of anyone checking out the Schmidts' house. "I went over to see Joe. He's doing okay. He says he can't wait to get back to work now that he doesn't have to catch 'critters.' "

She laughed. "Joe said 'critters?' "

"No, ma'am. The FCC frowns on using that kind of language on a cell phone. I can't tell you what he called them but he was mighty happy. And I never want to go out on patrol with Ed again. All he does is talk about Trudy!"

"I'm going to drop this hair sample off with Nick." She explained about the girls at the college. "Then I'll be back at the office. I want to run those three girls through the computer and see what we find."

"You got it!"

Sharyn stopped at the hospital, thinking she and Nick could also go to lunch while she was there but he wasn't in the morgue.

Megan looked up from a computer when she heard her. "Sheriff Howard."

"Megan." She glanced around. "Where's Nick?"

"The old man? He's out with Keith finding and classifying mold spores."

Sharyn took out Susan's hair sample. "I'd like to leave this here for him."

"A strand test? I can do that. I'm official now, you know."

"I know. Congratulations."

The girl shrugged her thin shoulders. "Yeah, well, it's more exciting than embalming. That's what I was planning to do."

"You—uh—just wanted to work with dead people?"

"Yeah. Pretty much." Megan took out the hair strand with a pair of tweezers and put it under a microscope. "This isn't DNA but I bet I can guess if it matches the other Blondie."

"Okay." Sharyn glanced uneasily around the empty morgue.

"Nope. No match. This one is natural. The hair texture is coarser too. Try again."

"Would you mind sending it off anyway?"

"No prob, mistress! I hear and I obey!"

"Thanks." Sharyn started back out the door.

"You don't like me, do you?"

"I think you're okay." Sharyn turned back towards her. "Did I say something that made you feel I didn't like you?"

Megan shrugged and looked away. "Nah. I was just wondering. Since we're gonna be working together from now on. It's good to know who hates you."

Keith and Nick came downstairs at that moment. They were juggling dozens of plastic bags full of dirt.

"Well, this is scary," Nick said. "My two favorite women standing here in the morgue talking."

"I came to take you out for lunch," Sharyn said, refusing to be drawn into that discussion.

Nick didn't pursue it. "Let me wash my hands."

Her cell phone rang. "Sheriff Howard."

"Cari's arrested a group of teenagers out at the subdivision," Ernie told her briefly. "We're going out there now."

"Okay. I'm on my way."

"What's up?" Nick questioned.

"Cari might have caught our burglars."

"I saw them sneaking in the side of the house," Cari told them when they arrived.

A media van from the local TV station was parked on John Schmidt's freshly laid grass. Foster Odom and his photographer were running up from their car.

"Marvella." Sharyn nodded towards the reporters. "Keep them away from the house."

"You got it, Sheriff!" Like a feisty bulldog, Marvella planted herself at the center of the drive and faced down the reporters. "Where do you think you're going?"

The Gazette's star reporter tried to push by her.

"Try that again and you'll end up in jail," she explained, rebuffing him.

Foster Odom pushed his worn Panthers cap back on his balding head. "Is that the gang that's been robbing the houses out here? Because if it is, the public has a right to know!"

"You got no rights here, sir, 'cept those I give you! Now step back!"

"She's good," Ernie observed with a satisfied grin.

Sharyn nodded and walked to the end of the concrete drive

where Cari had all four teenagers laying on their stomachs with their hands behind their heads. "What happened?"

"I observed them sneaking into the side of the house."

"Man, we weren't doing anything!" one of the boys said. "We were thinking about buying a house like this."

"Yeah," the boy next to him chimed in.

"Shut up and lay still!" Cari ordered.

Sharyn glanced at Ernie. He shrugged and walked up to the last of the four boys. "Come on, you. Let's go into the garage and have a talk."

"Stay here with these two, Cari," Sharyn said. "I'm going to talk to this one."

"Yes, ma'am. Would you like me to interrogate these two?"

"Not right now. Just watch them." Sharyn helped the boy to his feet. Unlike his two brazen counterparts, he was on the verge of tears. She took him up on the porch away from the group that was steadily growing on the street.

"It wasn't us, Sheriff," he told her quickly. "We were going into the house but we weren't gonna rob it. We were just looking for someplace out of the way to have a party. That's all."

"The doors were locked."

"I know."

"Why don't you tell me your name." She flipped open her notebook.

"Mason Rosemont."

She looked at him thoughtfully. "Julia Richmond's younger brother?"

"Yeah."

"Opening a locked door on someone else's property and going in is breaking and entering," she explained to him. "It doesn't matter whether you steal anything or not."

"We didn't rob anything."

Sharyn looked at the Nikes on his feet. "What size shoe do you wear?"

He glanced down. "Size ten."

"All right, Mason, before you tell me anything else, I think you should know that you have the right to an attorney. If you can't afford an attorney, one will be provided for you."

"You're arresting me?"

"I'm afraid so, son. Put your hands behind you. Don't make this any worse than it is already. You have the right to remain silent. If you choose to give up that right, anything you say can be used against you. Do you understand these rights?"

He wiped his nose on his sleeve. "Yeah. What's gonna happen?"

"You're coming with me to the sheriff's office."

"They're already reporting that you're arresting the Silver Dollar Gang," Trudy told them when they got back to the office with the four boys.

"Why do they call them that?" Sharyn asked, annoyed.

"Because they took a silver dollar collection from the first house they broke into," Trudy answered. "Sheriff, you have to keep up!"

Ernie chuckled. "Let's take these boys into the interrogation room."

Cari punched her right fist into the palm of her left hand. "I can get them to confess!"

"If there's nothing I can do, I'm going to take Marvella out on patrol and we're gonna drop by the shooting range," Ed told them.

"Go ahead,"Sharyn said. "We should be fine."

"I can stay and handle the press for you, Sheriff," Marvella offered.

"That's okay. Nobody's going anywhere for right now. All four of the boys have asked for lawyers. We'll sit tight until they get here."

When the boys were all seated at the big wooden table in the conference/interrogation room, Sharyn nodded to Ernie. "I'm going to have a talk with Cari."

He sighed. "All right. I guess what I'm saying isn't working."

"I'll be right back."

She motioned for Cari to join her in her office.

Cari closed the door on her way in then took a seat. "Don't worry, Sheriff. It was all part of a day's work."

Sharyn turned around abruptly and faced her. "You're fired. Get your things together and clean off your desk."

"What?" Cari asked faintly.

"You heard me! What do you think you were doing out there today? You recklessly endangered your life! What were you supposed to do if you saw anything suspicious?"

"Call for backup?"

"Is that what you did?"

"No, ma'am."

"I can't have a deputy who ignores my orders. You could've been killed out there because you wanted to prove how tough you are. I thought you were smarter than that!"

Cari gritted her teeth. "I was trying to do my job! I knew I could handle those boys!"

"There were four of them! You were lucky they didn't jump you!"

She shot to her feet. "I could've taken them!"

Sharyn got in her face. "No, you couldn't! They would've knocked you down and taken your gun away. If they didn't shoot you outright, they would've held you hostage."

"No! That couldn't happen to me again!"

"Yes, it could! You can't prove to me how tough you are, Deputy! Only how smart you are! What you did today was stupid! I don't want stupid people working for me! I've gone to enough funerals for dead law officers."

Cari's eyes widened. Her mouth opened but no sound came out. She sank down suddenly into her chair. "You don't understand."

"That's the problem. I do understand and I've let it go because of it. When I first started here, I barely knew how to shoot a gun. Everyone thought I wouldn't make it as sheriff. I knew I had to prove how tough I was."

"What happened?"

"One of the two men who killed my father shot me in the leg as I was chasing him. No backup. I would've bled to death except that Ernie was coming right behind me. He saved my life. Then he told me I was stupid and that he'd personally shoot me if I ever did anything so stupid again."

Cari shrugged. "I just wanted to protect myself."

"You do that by being smart, not by acting tough. Keep that in mind or I really will fire you."

"You weren't serious? I'm still a deputy?"

Sharyn sat down at her desk. "For now. I wanted to get your attention, Cari. But don't let anything like this happen again."

"No, ma'am. Thank you."

"Let's get set up to take statements from those boys. I'm sure it won't be too long before their lawyers are here."

"Do you think they're the Silver Dollar Gang?"

"No." She sighed. "I wish they were."

"The press—"

"I know."

The phone rang. "Sheriff Howard."

"Congratulations," The DA's voice boomed out over the line. "You got the Silver Dollar Gang."

"Thanks, sir, but I think that's premature. I don't think these are the right people."

"What do you mean? Weren't they breaking into the house?"

"Yes, sir. But they didn't have a van. They kicked open the door. The gang is more sophisticated. These are boys looking to get into trouble."

"And one of them is our newest commissioner's brother?"

Sharyn took a deep breath. "Yes, sir."

The door to her office slammed open. Julia Richmond stood in the entryway like an enraged queen.

"I'll have to call you back, sir. Ms. Richmond is here now." Sharyn put down the phone.

"Just what do you mean arresting my brother, Sheriff?"

"He was caught breaking into a house, ma'am. We had no choice."

"We'll see about that! You probably set this whole thing up to use as leverage of some sort because I'm threatening to change everything you do!"

Sharyn walked around Julia, sniffing her expensive perfume as she did. "Please come in and sit down, Ms. Richmond. You're right . . . in a way. I didn't plan to set this up but I've been thinking and it might not be a bad idea."

Julia was incensed. She flicked her sable-brown hair out of her face and tapped her foot. "I will *not* be blackmailed, Sheriff!"

"I wouldn't think of it, ma'am. If you'll allow me to explain."

The commissioner flounced to a chair and sat on the edge. "You have about two minutes before my lawyer rushes in here to see what's going on."

Sharyn sat opposite her. "I know your brother isn't part of the Silver Dollar Gang."

"You do?"

"But he was caught breaking into the house we set up for surveillance to catch the gang."

"And?" Julia asked suspiciously.

"I'd like to use him and his friends to catch the gang."

"How do you plan to do that, Sheriff?"

"By holding them here until the gang shows up again."

"You mean arresting them?"

"No. I mean holding them for their own protection, you could say. The gang would feel safe even though they'll know we were out there watching them. Your brother and his friends tipped them off and that makes our surveillance house useless. Unless the gang thinks we believe we have the group."

"I won't do it!" Julia shot to her feet.

"Then we'll have to arrest your brother and charge him with breaking into the house."

"You're going to arrest him anyway."

"Not technically. We'd hold him here but it wouldn't go against his record. And I wouldn't press charges against him or his friends for their cooperation."

Julia's dark eyes narrowed. "How long?"

"I'm not sure."

"This is Friday. I won't allow it past the weekend."

"All right. If the gang wants to make us look stupid, they should move pretty quickly. If not, we'll have to set up another surveillance house."

"And you'll drop all charges?"

"Yes."

"Maybe it will be good for Mason anyway. My parents have had nothing but trouble with him since last summer. I don't know what it is." Julia looked up at Sharyn. "I guess I should thank you for even offering."

"No need, ma'am. What they did spoiled our surprise but this might put it back right again. I appreciate your cooperation."

Julia put out her hand. "I'll talk to the boys and their parents. Goodness knows, I know all of them well enough and I think they all owe me money!"

"That's generous of you." Sharyn shook her hand. She couldn't help but compare Julia's dainty, manicured hand to her own callused, large one. She put her hands in her pockets.

"You aren't mad about the commission splitting the law enforcement duties, are you, Sheriff?"

"No, ma'am," Sharyn replied honestly. "I'm looking forward to a vacation."

"With the crime rate growing every day, I don't think that will happen very often. But it will free you up to spend more time on the important things. We used to have a murder here every so often, remember? I'm not saying it's your fault. I just want to feel safe again. This department is too strained to go on like it has. I'm glad you appreciate that fact."

"Yes, ma'am." In truth, Sharyn was amazed at the woman's perception. She wasn't the empty-headed socialite so many people took her for.

"Well, I'll let you go back to work catching these thieves. Good luck, Sheriff."

"Thanks."

Sharyn told Ernie to let Julia and the boys' parents into the interrogation room to talk to their prisoners. "I hope it works."

"If not, we'll have to start over. I hope you're right about letting these boys go. Otherwise, they might be the Silver Dollar Gang a few years from now."

"Maybe Julia will be right and staying here a few nights will straighten them out."

"Maybe," he agreed reluctantly. "I guess the only question now is, what do you say to the press?"

Chapter Eight

Sharyn straightened her spine and decided against wearing her hat. She ran her hand carelessly through her copper-colored curls. Then she walked out of her office to address the crowd of reporters who squeezed into the main part of the building to hear what she had to say. There was no live feed. All cameras were left outside in the cold. Ernie, Trudy and Cari stood at the back of the room. Ernie gave Sharyn a thumb's up.

"Good afternoon. I have a favor to ask of all of you."

There was a groan and some foot shuffling.

"What's up, Sheriff?" Foster Odom demanded first.

"I need some cooperation. It has to do with catching the Silver Dollar Gang."

That brought an eruption of questions from the 10 reporters who were waiting.

"What do you mean, Sheriff? Don't you have the gang in custody?"

"No. And our surveillance house has been compromised by what happened. The only way to save it now is if you're willing to help me out."

Odom smacked his chewing gum. "What do you need?"

"I need you to run the story that we caught the gang. That they're being processed and arraigned. If the real gang believes it, we're still in business. I think they'll make a quick move to show us how dumb we are. If not, it won't matter.

They'll probably clear out with everything they've stolen and we'll never catch them."

"What about the print you got at last week's scene?" one of the reporters asked.

"You should ask the ME about that but as far as I know, it hasn't shown up in any databases yet. We might be a day or two away from catching these people if you're willing to help."

"You and Nick not speaking after your fling with the senator?" one reporter threw out while the others chuckled.

"If we could keep this on the subject, please."

There was a lot of muttering and complaining but in the end, they all knew they were going to work with her. They covered crime in the area. If they lost faith with the sheriff's office, it could mean their jobs.

"All right," Odom agreed for the Gazette. "What do you want us to say?"

Sharyn exhaled, not realizing how nervous she was that they wouldn't agree. "All I want you to say is that we have the gang in custody and that we're moving towards a speedy trial. We'll see what happens after that."

"Can we report the boys' names? What are you going to do with them while you wait to see what happens?"

"You know better. All four boys are juveniles. And we'll hold all of them here until the weekend is over. If nothing comes up by then, we'll let them go."

"What about Mason Rosemont? Is Julia Richmond going along with this?" Odom asked.

"They have my full support." Julia sailed forward to stand beside Sharyn. She clasped her hands in front of her. "We only want to do what we can to right this terrible situation."

"What about your brother, Commissioner? Will he be held responsible for anything in this?"

"We'll discuss those details after the weekend," Sharyn said. "I appreciate all of you working with this office."

"What about you and the senator?" the reporter from WXLZ asked boldly. "What's happening with that?"

"You know I don't talk about my private life," she joked, refusing to let anyone see her run scared on that rumor. With any luck, it would die a quick death.

The group began to break up. Odom moved closer to Sharyn and Julia. "Is it true you two are getting into a catfight over the separation between the county and the town law enforcement? I think you owe me an answer on that anyway."

Julia raised her chin. "Does it look like we're fighting, Mr. Odom?"

"No, ma'am." He grinned. "But looks can be deceiving. Can I have a quote from each of you so my readers can tell for themselves?"

Julia glanced at Sharyn then took the first step. "My proposal to separate the city and county law enforcement didn't come about because I feel that what Sheriff Howard is doing isn't working. It came about because she's wasted on so many small things around here that would be better off being handled by people with less experience. That would free her to work on the really hard cases."

Odom looked at Sharyn.

She wasn't sure what she could say that would sound as complimentary. "When I heard about the separation idea, I wasn't offended. If anything, I was relieved. We're long past due on upgrading our system in the city and county. There's too much happening here for a handful of deputies to handle adequately."

The reporter nodded. "Fair enough. Mind if I take a picture of the two of you?"

His photographer took a quick shot. "Thanks."

"Any thoughts on who might be chosen to head up the city version of the police unit?" he asked Julia.

"Not as yet."

Sharyn looked at the other woman. She knew that she was lying. Was it as obvious to Odom?

"Thanks for letting us in on the secret, Sheriff."

"Thank you for your help, Mr. Odom."

When the reporters were gone, Julia sagged visibly. She sat

down hard in a chair and took a glass of water from her personal assistant. "I hate reporters."

Sharyn laughed. "Let's hope they can do something to help for a change."

"The other parents agreed," Julia told her. "Actually, getting my mom and dad to agree was the hardest part."

"No one likes to admit that they're kids have gone wrong," Ernie said.

She smiled at him. "I know. That's why I'm glad I don't have any! Call me if you hear anything, Sheriff."

"Of course."

"Well, well!" Ernie said when Julia was gone with a whiff of perfume and her PA following close behind. "She's not what I expected."

"She's grown up for sure," Trudy observed.

"I guess having money and power can be good for some people," Sharyn agreed. "But I think we're not going to like the commission's choice to run the Diamond Springs police department."

"Why do you say that?" Ernie asked.

"Because she just lied about not knowing who she wants to head it up. And I think she was lying for my benefit, not Odom's."

"Great!"

"Not much we can do about it. We'll have to learn to work with whoever it is. Is the surveillance equipment still set up at the house?"

Ernie nodded. "We're ready to rock and roll! Do you want someone posted out there again?"

"I don't think so. Let's wait and see what happens. The gang will be looking hard for anything like that. I don't want to give it away. If we catch them on tape, that should be enough."

The phone rang and Trudy called out, "Selma on line two, Sheriff."

"Just tell her I'm on my way," Sharyn told her.

"Where are you off to?" Ernie wondered.

"I'm going to see Sam today. Think you can handle it until I get back?"

Ernie laughed. "I'm getting married next week. I think I can handle anything if I can handle *that!*"

"Let me know if anything happens."

"You know I will. In the meantime, I'm gonna be checking out what I can find on those girls from Piper."

"Thanks, Ernie."

Unionville was the county seat for Union County, North Carolina. It boasted an impressive new courthouse and a new jail that was about three blocks away. Sharyn knew from their experience in Diamond Springs how sorry they were going to be that they didn't build them together.

She and Selma parked beside a towering statue of an angel with a sword pointing at the heavens. She was carrying a slain soldier's body across one of her arms. It marked the city's involvement in the Confederacy.

It was said to be the resting place of several soldiers' bodies, among them Captain William Pierce who saved the town from being razed by Union troops. The area didn't see much fighting on the whole. But after some skirmishes to the east, Union soldiers followed a ragtag group of Confederate soldiers, ferreting them out of their hiding places as they went. The tale said that no one was spared as they used fire and sword to bring them to Yankee justice.

"That statue gives me the willies," Selma said, drawing her heavy shawl closer against the cold. "Why would they want to keep it here?"

"To remember what happened."

"It was a long time ago. How could they expect to heal the breach between the north and south with things like that hanging around?"

Sharyn laughed. "I didn't know you weren't a fan of the Confederacy?"

"I'm not a fan of any violence. Especially, stupid violence!"

They walked together across the parking lot towards the jail.

"How did it go with the professor telling Chief Murray about the knife?"

Selma shrugged. "The chief wasn't happy about it. But I think he can make his case against Sam anyway. Sam was in Professor Neal's office with me. He could have seen the knife and come back for it."

"I was afraid it would be that way."

"Any news from your end?"

"Not yet. Ernie's checking out Lynette's friends. They're a pretty tight clique."

"But that doesn't mean they knew anything about Lynette's murder."

"Unless she was seeing someone they aren't telling us about."

Selma's face lit up hopefully. "I hope that's true."

The jail was modern and well lit. Computers ran everything. They were greeted at the entrance by two guards who gave them IDs. Then they were buzzed through to the back of the building where prisoners were allowed to see friends and relatives.

Sharyn used her status as a visiting law enforcement officer to get them a private meeting with Sam. The county still only gave them 20 minutes. They waited for 10 of them while he was brought up from his cell.

When they were finally allowed into the room, Sam was chained to the floor with both his hands in cuffs and his ankles in leg irons. A guard waited outside the locked door.

"Sam!" Selma rushed to him and hugged him tightly.

Sharyn looked the other way. She felt awkward watching her aunt kiss him. It was something like going through her aunt's personal papers would be.

"Sharyn," Sam greeted her. "I'm pleased to see you. Jeff told me about everything you've done for me. I appreciate your help."

She turned back and sat down in a chair at the tiny table. "I'm glad you're better."

He touched the fading yellow bruises on his face. "I don't know. I think I looked better in purple."

Selma laughed and crouched beside him. "Is there anything you need? Anything we can get you?"

"Out of here?"

Sharyn frowned. This wasn't helping. They didn't have a lot of time and she had a lot of questions. "Sam, I know everyone's asked you about what you remember."

"Yeah. And I wish I had a new answer for you."

"You still don't remember anything?"

He squinted his dark eyes. "I remember going over to the shrubs. I thought an animal was injured. The noise wasn't like a human noise. Someone ran away when they heard me."

"How many?" Sharyn sat forward in her chair.

"I'm not sure. At least three."

"Did you notice anything out of the ordinary? Any smells or sounds after you got to the girl's body?"

Sam closed his eyes and thought back. "I could smell her blood. It has a smell, you know. Especially at night when it mingles with the earth. She was wearing perfume. There was more than one kind of perfume. And the smell of cigarette smoke. She looked at me. She tried to speak. I knelt beside her, almost on the knife. That's when I picked it up. When it was in my hands, I could feel its power."

"The knife?"

He opened his eyes and stared at her. "Yes. It's steeped in evil. From a hundred deaths. I couldn't see it but I *knew*."

"Knew what, Sam?" Selma asked in a frightened voice.

"I knew it was *s-gi-na*. I knew it had come back to me."

Sharyn cleared her throat, trying not to be drawn into the spell of his voice and his strange intonation. "You mean it was yours before the killing?"

"Not mine alone. It belonged to my people. It was lost. I heard a sound like giggling and then the dogs baying in the distance."

"Why didn't you run, Sam?" Sharyn wondered. "Why didn't you try to get away?"

He shrugged. His eyes were misted and far away. "It wouldn't do any good. It would find me again. Better to stay and face it. Maybe that way it would be destroyed before it could kill again."

Selma glanced at Sharyn uneasily. "Sam, where did you see the knife before?'

"I didn't. I *knew* of its existence."

"Did you know the girl, Lynette Ashe?"

"Yes. I took her down to Diamond Springs a couple of times to visit her boyfriend. She didn't have a car and I was headed that way. It wasn't a big deal. And I'm always a fan of true love."

Sharyn felt her breath catch in her chest. She'd bet Chief Murray knew that too. No doubt Susan, and Lynette's other friends, told him. It gave Sam ties with both girls that were killed. Even if they could clear him of Lynette's death, she wasn't sure they could clear him of Becky Taylor's death. There were no suspects on that case. Sam dropped into the slot convincingly.

Looking at his eyes and listening to him, he seemed a likely suspect to her. If it were her case, she'd consider it as closed as the chief. "Sam, was Becky Taylor killed with that knife too?"

"Becky?" He frowned over the name. "I remember her from the animal camp! She was a nice girl. Used to laugh a lot. I don't know. It's possible. The knife has been used to kill many women."

Selma wrapped her shawl closer like she was cold.

Sam's gaze sharpened. "But if you're asking me if I killed either of them, no. I didn't kill Becky or Lynette. If I had any time with that knife, I'd destroy it. It shouldn't be allowed to exist."

Sharyn took the moment to point out the obvious to him. "You can see how bad this looks for you. You knew both girls. You were found with Lynette on the scene. Have you told the police what you've told us about the knife?"

"Yes! I was hoping they'd destroy it. Where is it now?"

"At the police station in Rock Springs," Selma answered. "Unless they've already brought it out here for your trial."

The guard came into the room. "Time's up, Sheriff."

"Thanks." Sharyn got to her feet.

"Thank you for coming, Sheriff," Sam said, trying to extend his hand and finding his movement hampered by the chain. "I'm sorry I can't make it."

"That's okay." She moved close to him and shook his hand. "You've got a good lawyer, Sam. Listen to her. I'm sure she doesn't want you saying things about this knife to anyone else."

"I will, Sharyn. Good-bye, Selma. I'm sorry you had to go through this."

Selma kissed him hard on the mouth and fled from the room.

Sharyn followed her as the guard closed himself in the room with Sam. She found Selma crying on a wooden bench in the hallway. "Are you okay?"

Selma stared up at her. "He did it, didn't he?"

Sharyn sat down beside her. "I don't think so. He has this weird idea about the knife, but I don't believe he killed either of those girls."

"Why? He *sounds* crazy!"

"I know."

"When they put him on the stand during the trial, he'll convict himself."

"If it gets that far, let's hope Ms. Farmer is smart enough not to do that."

"He sounded so bad, Sharyn. I never—" Selma collected herself and wiped her eyes with the back of her hand. "We have to find out who did these things if you really believe that it wasn't Sam."

Sharyn hugged her. "Don't you believe anymore?"

"I don't know what to believe."

Their drive back to the college was silent and strained. Sharyn was almost relieved when she let her aunt out at her door.

"Thanks for going with me," Selma said. "I wish it was better news."

"Don't give up yet. If Sam was unhinged and didn't mind telling us about the knife and the evil spirit, he wouldn't mind telling us that he killed those girls either. There's someone else, Aunt Selma. Let's keep digging."

"I will. Thank you, Sharyn. Have I told you yet what a very fine law officer you are? And how proud your father would be of you?"

Sharyn smiled and glanced down at the steering wheel. "I hope that means I can help Sam."

"I hope so too. I'll call if I learn anything else."

"Love you, Aunt Selma."

"I love you too, Sharyn."

But before Sharyn could leave the tiny college town, Chief Murray flagged her down. She pulled close to him at the curb, not wanting to get out, and rolled down her window.

"Fine day," he said, squinting up into the sunlight. "A mite cold but fine otherwise."

"I don't think you stopped me to comment on the weather, Chief."

"You're right, Sharyn. By now, I'm sure you know of Mr. Two Rivers' involvement with Lynette."

"You mean that he was taking her to Diamond Springs to see her boyfriend?"

The chief laughed. "Is that what he told you? Bless his heart, he don't know if he's coming or going! No, ma'am, I mean the part where he was *personally* involved with Miss Ashe. He was taking her to *his* house in Diamond Springs."

"You have proof of that?"

"Yes, ma'am, I do. Her friends finally 'fessed up to it. They saw them together doing romantic things several times. They told us originally that she was going to see Tim Stryker. But then they told the truth."

"I've spoken with those girls, Chief. I don't think they'd know the truth if it bit them!"

He shrugged. "You and I both know this case is closed, all

but the sentencing. It would be better for Mr. Two Rivers if he'd confess and save us all a trial. It will be nice to be able to look both those little girls' families in the eyes and be able to tell them that the man who killed their daughters is going to die for his crimes. I'm sorry he's a friend of yours. Maybe you need to take a closer look at your friends, hmm?"

"I have to get back to work, Chief," Sharyn said, tired of his gloating. "Good luck with your case."

Chief Murray laughed. "Don't need luck, Sharyn. I got truth on my side!"

She nodded and rolled up her window as she drove away. She couldn't help but feel Officer Kaiser's eyes on her as she was talking with the Chief. The two men belonged in this strange little town.

Her cell phone rang when she was almost back to Diamond Springs. It was Sam's brother.

"I can't get away from this trial until they let me go, Sharyn. But I really need to see you. Can I meet you somewhere tonight? Probably the soonest I can get there will be ten or so. I wouldn't ask if it wasn't important."

"All right. I'll meet you at the sheriff's office."

"Thanks."

She closed her cell phone, wondering what he could want to say to her that couldn't be said over the phone. She went over and over what Sam said to her as she drove. If he wasn't crazy, then he was establishing something of what she guessed happened. At least three people leaving the scene. Giggling. The scent of different kinds of perfume and cigarette smoke.

If she was right, then Lynette's friends followed her outside the dorm when she went to smoke and attacked her with the knife they took from the professor. Did they take the knife from him because she was his favorite? Were they fighting about splitting up the profits of their robberies?

Nothing but the barest of hunches took her to those conclusions. Susan's blond hair. Her muscular body. The amount of electronic gadgets in Lynette's dorm room. The girls' manner when they talked to Selma. It would be nicer to have some hard evidence but until something broke, that wasn't legally possible.

If the gang, minus Lynette, took her bait and went into John Schmidt's house so they got them on tape, they could work towards uncovering something more of Lynette's murder. Even if it was by accident while they were investigating the details of the robberies.

It wouldn't do any good to get any evidence without a search warrant. If they found something incriminating, they wouldn't be able to use it in a trial. But if they found it while they were looking for evidence of another crime that would be a whole different can of worms!

Charlie waved her in at the gate to the impound lot.

Ernie met her at the back door. "How'd it go?"

"Not good." She told him about everything Sam said. "He looked so weird. It was like he was telling a story or something. I could feel chills running down my spine."

"Poor old Sam. He's got himself in a fix. I wish I could say what I found helped him."

"Susan Atmore?"

"Yeah. She's a good student. Good grades, good parents. She was arrested in her last year of high school for shoplifting. The store pressed charges. She took a sequined pocketbook. Otherwise, she's as clean as mountain air. Hasn't been in any trouble since she came to Piper."

"What about the other girls?" Sharyn asked as she went into her office.

"They're the same except no previous records at all. Including Lynette."

"And if we suspected Susan because she was picked up for shoplifting, we'd have to go and get Kristie too?"

Ernie nodded as he followed her into the office. "Yep."

"What are we missing?" she asked him, sitting down. "Sam told me he didn't run away because he wanted to destroy the knife because it's evil. From his account, it sounds like Lynette was outside smoking and someone jumped her. Maybe all four of them. It would make sense so that none of them could tell."

"You think her girlfriends did it? I thought you liked them for our Silver Dollar Gang? Isn't that why you had Nick check her hair and thumbprint?"

"Yeah."

"I know you're not thinking these good, smart girls not only conceived and engineered a serious of sophisticated burglaries, they also killed their friend."

"I don't know. There's nothing linking them together. But they did have access to the knife, as much as Sam did. And if they were involved in the burglaries together, maybe they had an argument. Maybe Lynette wanted more of a cut."

Ernie grinned his lopsided grin. "The robberies *are* all on that side of the county. Of course, there could be a size twelve pair of Nikes in Lynette's closet that the Chief wouldn't think to take away since they wouldn't pertain to her murder."

Sharyn lay back in her chair and stared at the ceiling. "Maybe. We could do with a break like that. But we couldn't get in there to check it out until we have them for the robberies. If I'm wrong and the gang isn't those girls, I'm afraid there's no hope for Sam."

"He's in a bad place for sure. A lot like I was. But you pulled my bacon out of the fire."

"Good thing too. Because Annie would've flayed me if you'd ended up in jail."

Ernie's smile faded. "About the other night when I was having second thoughts about getting married—"

Sharyn's blue eyes widened. "When was that?"

"Thanks. You're a pretty good friend, you know?"

"Yeah. I know. You too."

Nick brought lunch for them both and they shared it on her desk. "I can't believe you're still looking at Susan Atmore for the break-ins."

"Why?" Sharyn asked after swallowing a piece of her pickle. "Just because her hair doesn't match up?"

"And the thumbprint I have isn't hers."

"That doesn't mean it couldn't belong to Lynette."

He stared at her. "Is that where you're going with this?"

"Maybe." She took another bite of her cheese hoagie. "Can you check that out next?"

"Sure. I'll need a strand of hair from Lynette. I should be able to scrounge her thumbprints from the state."

"They've already taken her body back to Ohio. Do you think Bobby Fisher saved some of her hair?"

He munched a chip. "Probably not. I'll give him a call anyway. But if I could get into her dorm room, I might be able to find something."

"How would we know it was hers?"

"If it came from her hairbrush or from her underwear. Of course we could match skin cell DNA to hair DNA."

Sharyn raised her brows. "We'd never get a warrant on what I have right now. We'll have to wait until we get something more.

He nodded. "I'd like to see those Nikes."

"Yeah. Me too.

"Your mother called me this morning and told me how sorry she was that you preferred Senator Winter to me but that it was for the best."

Sharyn put down her sandwich. "What?"

He smiled. "She was very gracious about it. She offered to fix me up with one of your cousins."

"Which one?"

"Carol Ann or Carol Faye. I'm not sure which."

She laughed. "I think you'd do fine with either one."

"I'm glad you find this amusing."

"If I took it seriously, I'd have to go up to Raleigh and shoot him."

"That's my girl!" He offered her his pickle. "I heard you got Cari straightened out by telling her about getting shot."

She took his pickle and put it on her paper plate. "Nothing around here is sacred."

"Not like it was a secret! We all know what happened."

She shook her head. "Was Cari impressed?"

"I think so. She thought you were bulletproof. Or at least that your magical bracelets would protect you from bullets."

Sharyn finished her soda and wrapped up the last of her sandwich. "I'm going to miss these little lunches when I'm off in the county somewhere and you're here at the morgue."

His eyes got serious. "Is that what's going to happen?"

"I don't know. Julia hasn't shared that part of the plan with me yet."

"Are you worried about it?"

"No, not really. I think it would be good to separate the two aspects of crime around here. It would keep us from checking on every speeder and jaywalker in Diamond Springs."

"Any hint who'll head up the police for the city?"

"Nope. Are *you* worried?"

"Nope. I just got a big raise and two assistants that I know aren't homicidal maniacs. Or at least I don't think they are. I'm not sure yet about Megan. I can work with anyone."

"You didn't think you could work with me," she reminded him.

He got to his feet and took her hand, drawing her slowly up to face him. "I didn't think I could work with you without doing this." He kissed her. "Or this." He ran his fingers through her hair. "And I thought you might shoot me."

She smiled at him. "Oh, was that all? Why didn't you say so? I have this kind of relationship with several DAs, a few senators and a deputy or two. What's another ME?"

He squeezed her close against his chest. "Have I ever told you that they teach medical examiners several ways to kill difficult sheriffs without leaving any clues behind?"

"Have I ever told you that I love it when you're jealous?"

"Jealous?" Nick kissed her again. "Look who's talking!"

Ernie coughed from his vantage place at the doorway. "Much as I hate to break up any relationship that could eventually lead to marriage because the institution is one I prize highly, I need to see the sheriff. Then you two can do whatever you like."

"I have to go anyway. I have a thumbprint to look for." He looked at Ernie. "So are you going to break into the school?"

"Not unless you're there with me!"

"That's gonna happen! I'm looking forward to the party tomorrow night though. I haven't been to a bachelor party in years."

"Nobody you know brave enough to take the plunge?"

Nick shrugged. "Nobody I know who knows anyone they can imagine spending the rest of their life with. But I love bachelor parties. The beer, the stale pretzels. The lies."

"Yeah. You're getting the best end of the deal. Cari told me that Annie got some French movie called *Endearing Stranger* for them to watch after they open the gifts and talk about what a bad husband I'm going to make."

Nick patted Ernie's shoulder. "Cheer up! I have Wanda the bubble dancer coming tomorrow night."

Ernie laughed. "Isn't she about sixty now? I think she was there for my graduation from high school!"

Nick checked his pockets and found her business card. "Maybe this is her daughter."

"I can't believe I let you talk me into this." Sharyn moaned. "As many times as we've busted the Stag Inn Doe, the sheriff's department is having a party there! I hope the media doesn't find out!"

"A French film with subtitles is starting to look pretty good, huh?" Trudy leaned around the door. "Line one Sheriff. It's Mr. Percy."

Chapter Nine

Sharyn spent about an hour in DA Percy's office explaining her plan to catch the Silver Dollar Gang. He sat with his hands steepled up to his face. His eyes were closed. His head, covered with an obvious brown toupee, was thrown back against the padded headrest of his chair. His white linen suit and white shirt were creaseless and fresh as always. The man looked like he stepped out of a dry cleaner's ad.

Though she knew Percy was part of the good old boy network in Diamond Springs, he was different than his predatory predecessor Jack Winter. He was a courteous, old fashioned, southern gentleman. He never made her feel like he was about to devour her. And if he was looking over her shoulder, he was discreet about it.

She was nearly grateful to have him there after the last few years with the old DA. But she didn't let her guard down with him. She knew he might be even more dangerous since she could *almost* trust him. The parable of the scorpion and the frog came to mind.

The changes in the DA's office reflected his personality. His ADA was refreshingly honest and not so cutthroat as the people Jack Winter employed. He had a cheery-faced secretary who smiled at her as she came up to the door.

The air of double-dealing and back-room politics evaporated with the shift in office décor. The crystal liquor decanters Winter enjoyed so much were gone. Everyone knew that Percy

never touched a drop of spirits. The opulent curtains and furniture were out. Percy's tastes were simpler, though probably
not less expensive. There were pictures of his wife, children,
and grandchildren on his desk. Everything was easier, laid
back. Like the man himself.

Which brought her back to her present predicament. When
she was finished outlining her plan, Sharyn waited for a few
minutes. There was no response, no change in his position.
Was he asleep? She shifted in her chair. He didn't move. She
cleared her throat loudly. Nothing changed. She didn't want
to leave him sleeping in his office. Maybe she should call his
secretary?

He opened his eyes and looked at her. "I'm awake, Sheriff.
I heard every word. I was giving you my full attention. I think
the plan seems sound. I wish you'd confided in me sooner but
I know that takes some trust in our working relationship that
we haven't developed yet. I'm sure that will come."

"Thank you, sir."

His dark eyes studied her. "You're a very brave young
woman."

Sharyn glanced around the room. "I-uh—"

"Standing up to Jack Winter. Taking on possible dents to
your reputation. Challenging the police in other towns."

"Sir?"

"Did you think Chief Murray wouldn't complain about you
investigating a murder in his jurisdiction? He was explicit
about you overstepping your bounds of authority since it is
another county."

"I wasn't actually investigating, sir. More like checking into
the affair. I've tried to be discreet. And most of what I've
done and seen was with Chief Murray's permission. But he
and his assistant have gaping holes in their case, Mr. Percy. I
don't want Sam Two Rivers to go to prison for their eagerness
to solve the crime. And every time I do anything for him, I
take the time from my vacation. I keep a log. I'm not shirking
my duties to Diamond Springs."

Percy laughed. "I have no doubt! If you were any less honest, Sheriff, you couldn't stand up to Jack because he would've found something on you already and you'd be on his payroll."

Sharyn wanted to ask him if *he* was on Jack's payroll. Or vice versa. But she knew better. Her grandfather always said that the roots of the tree of evil went down too deep to dig up. You had to chop it down. It was a little flowery but it seemed apt in this case. "Well, I appreciate the compliment, sir. I do the best I can."

"I know you do. But maybe you could do a little less in Union County, hmm? I'd hate to see them file something against you with the state and tarnish that sterling reputation you prize so highly."

"Yes, sir."

"Good luck, Sheriff. Keep me posted. I believe you're doing a fine job."

"Yes, sir."

Sharyn walked towards the door. Eldeon Percy watched her carefully, never taking his eyes from her straight spine and the proud tilt of her head. She closed the sturdy portal behind her.

"She's a fighter." Jack Winter emerged from the hidden side room.

"She'll be the death of you," Percy observed. "Leave her alone, Jack. You don't need that kind of trouble."

Jack smiled and sat in the chair she vacated. "Everyone needs *that* kind of trouble, Percy. You're getting old if you don't think so. Besides, I can handle her. You'll see."

Sharyn waited at the office for Jefferson Two Rivers until almost midnight. JP and David were out on patrol. The new janitor was cleaning the desks in the main office. He was whistling a Christmas carol. It seemed like a long time since Christmas to her.

She had a nice dinner with Nick then went to the 'Y' to work out for an hour before coming back to the office. Her muscles were still twitching as she sat in her chair.

Nick laughed when she asked him if he wanted to come along and work out with her. "The only workout I do is on the firing range every weekend. And to prepare for that, I'm going home to grade tests. That red pen strengthens my trigger finger."

Sharyn worried about their differences and wondered how much longer their relationship could possibly last. Both of them were already months past their records with other people. She liked being with Nick, liked the way he made her feel. Would it last like Ernie and Annie? Who knew?

She finished catching up on her paperwork by 11 then watched some CNN. She thought about moving out of her office when the commission finally divided up the law enforcement duties. Would they find the sheriff's department a new home or put the police department in the courthouse? They had lots of room in the cavernous pink granite hulk.

She wasn't going to fight about it either way. There were too many important battles that she needed to win. Like getting the commission to create a new animal control department. She wouldn't waste time on one that didn't matter. No matter what, she'd still be the sheriff for the next four years and Diamond Springs would still be her home. That was enough.

Maybe her father would be disappointed in her. Maybe her grandfather's picture would scowl down at her with a little extra fervor if they were moved to another location. Both of them did their job from this office. But being sheriff for the last two years and getting past her father's death taught her one thing. She had to do what was right for her.

Which brought her back to the problem of moving out on her own. There would never be a good time to do it. Not in her mother's eyes. Hadn't she thought Sharyn should move up to the Capitol with her and Caison when they were going to be married? Faye would always find some reason for her to live at home.

She was just as sure that she should find her own place. When the house was done would be a good spot to jump off.

She was already in the apartment. It was furnished. She could bring her stuff over from the house but she wouldn't have to look for other furniture right away. It seemed perfect to her. Except that she was going to have to hurt her mother to do it.

She didn't like the idea of leaving Faye alone. After T. Raymond's death, it was unthinkable. But so much had changed since then. And Faye was bound to consider marrying Caison again after they were together for a while. How long would she actually be alone anyway?

"Sheriff?" The new janitor caught her attention by rapping on her door. "The door's buzzing. I think someone wants to come in!"

"Thanks!" Sharyn shook herself from her reveries and pushed the button to let Jefferson Two Rivers in the front door.

"Thanks for waiting." He shook her hand. "I'm sorry I'm so late. Between that murder trial and handling stuff that comes up at the office, I might as well not have a life at all. My kids call me their invisible father. My wife is threatening to find someone else who has a normal job."

"I know what you mean." She sat down behind her desk. "I don't have a husband or kids but the job is demanding. Coffee?"

"No, thanks. That's why I appreciate the time you've taken with helping Sam." Sheriff Two Rivers closed the door to her office and took a chair opposite her. "I know how hard it is. I'm afraid what I have to tell you makes it even worse."

Sharyn shook her head wearily. Her brain felt numbed by all the things against Sam. Clearing his name seemed hopeless. "I don't see how it could be. I saw him today. His 'other worldliness' works for what he normally does protecting animals. Telling me and everyone else about the evil knife he can't escape is going to send him straight to Raleigh. They could decide to ask for the death penalty on this case."

Jefferson slumped in his chair. "I know. But it's true. What Sam said about the knife. All of it is true."

She sat forward. "What are you saying?"

He took out the wrinkled fax she sent him. "This knife belongs to my people."

"The Cherokee?"

"Not just the Cherokee. We are part of the Eastern band that remained behind during the enforced move to Oklahoma. Our ancestors hid in caves and hollows in the forest until the army was done looking for them. They came together slowly, keeping a low profile for many years. They never trusted the government again but eventually, they emerged as the Cherokee nation most here know today. Singers, storytellers, casino owners. Sam and I are part of all of that. It is our heritage."

"And the knife?"

"The first story I heard about the knife was from my great-great-grandmother. A man was filled with a dark spirit. He created a knife that could be used to fulfill the spirit's purpose. It killed many Cherokee women who were in hiding. Many more later." He pointed to the paper. "This knife."

"How can you tell it's the same knife?"

He showed her the faint scratching on the handle. "This glyph is for my mother's tribe. Hawk tribe. These other marks are the record of the dead that this knife has killed."

Sharyn drew in a deep breath when she saw the number of lines. "Did Sam have this knife?"

"No. We haven't seen it in our tribe for a long time. It was lost during the time of your civil war. The last time it surfaced, it killed three women. That was probably over a hundred years ago."

"If I were a lawyer, I'd wonder what the odds would be of it turning up in Sam's hand while he was standing over a dead woman. But I'd also take into consideration that it was stolen from Professor Neal's office."

"Yeah. So would I." Jefferson looked at the picture of the knife. "We heard the stories about it so many times, Sam and I would know it anywhere. If I touched it in the dark, I would know its feel. I would know its evil."

"*S-gi-na.*"

"Yes."

Sharyn shook herself. It was late and she was tired. Fantasy was easy to entertain under those circumstances but it wouldn't help save Sam's life. "This knife was stolen from a collector who lives at Piper College. We can't prove Sam took it but they can't prove that he did either. This evidence isn't much worse. There are lots of Cherokee artifacts. That's pretty general even if it belonged to your clan."

"You don't understand. It corrupts every man it touches. It doesn't belong in a museum. It should be destroyed."

"Jefferson, are you saying Sam killed those girls because the knife made him evil and he couldn't help it?"

"Maybe."

She took a deep breath. "That's not reasonable."

"No it isn't. But evil isn't reasonable. That doesn't mean it doesn't exist."

"So we stop trying to find the real truth and help Sam because this knife says it all?"

"No." He covered his face with his hands. "I don't know."

"Look." Sharyn grabbed hold of what little sanity there was in that room. "You're exhausted. This information isn't going to help Sam. If the DA finds out about it, it will only add to the mountain of evidence against him. Especially since they seem so convinced that both girls were killed with it. It's bad. But I may have an alternative answer. At least to the last killing. If we can dismantle that case, we might be able to get at the first one. Don't give up yet."

His black eyes were desperate when he raised them to her. "I want to help Sam. I want him to be innocent. I didn't know this knife was involved. No matter what, it has to be destroyed. When the trial is over, the collector has to be convinced to destroy it."

She nodded solemnly. "I'll do the best I can."

"Where is it now?"

"Either at the police station in Rock Springs or waiting for the trial in Unionville. I'm not sure."

He sighed and pulled himself out of the chair. "I should go. It's a long way home."

She was glad to have him talking normally again. "You're welcome to stay the night here and drive back in the morning."

"My wife would be worried even more then. Not only would I be ignoring her, I'd be spending the night with a red-headed lady sheriff!"

"Okay. But be careful. I'll let you know what happens."

"Thanks." He shook her hand again. "I'll never forget what you tried to do for Sam."

She clutched his hand tightly. "I'm not giving up on him yet. You shouldn't either!"

"Are you so sure evil doesn't exist?" he demanded. "Is there nothing in the shadows but stillness? Have you never heard a footstep when you were alone in a room?"

Sharyn wasn't sure how to answer his questions. It wasn't that she didn't believe that anything was possible. She just refused to believe that an evil knife could make a good man murder someone. She watched his Suburban pull away from the curb and disappear into the darkness. She hoped he would make it home.

She walked the quiet streets of Diamond Springs towards her apartment. She could smell the fresh bread baking at the bakery on 4th Street. An owl hooted then swooped across the sky overhead, diving towards the lake. She heard a noise behind her and glanced around. There was no one there. Shaking her head at her own level of susceptibility, she let herself into the apartment and locked the door behind her.

Sharyn was off the next day. Her only Saturday a month. She planned on sleeping late since she was going to Ernie's bachelor party that night, but her mother woke her at seven.

"Wake up, lazy bones! I thought we'd get to have a nice chat this morning since I saw on the calendar that you were off today. Maybe we could see a movie together or go shopping."

Sharyn sat up slowly, not really awake. "Uh-sure."

"And I made some blueberry pancakes! Your favorite."

Actually, they hadn't been her favorite since she was 12 but she didn't have the heart to tell her mother. So when Faye was going to do something special, she made blueberry pancakes. "Uh-thanks."

"Hurry and get your shower now! And do something with your hair! You're a mess!"

Sharyn staggered in and out of the shower. She ran her fingers through her curls when they were dry then yawned as she put on black sweat pants and sweater. She pushed her feet into fuzzy yellow slippers she got for her birthday from Aunt Selma.

Faye made a huge affair out of putting pancakes on both their plates then putting a small cruet of warm blueberry syrup in the center of the table. "These are just the way you like them, Sharyn. Crispy edges, soft middles."

"Thanks, Mom."

Faye sat down, wiping her hands on her apron. "Well, eat up!"

Sharyn sipped her coffee and ate a few bites of her pancakes. She glanced at her pretty mother with her flowered apron and perfect hair and make-up. Now was as good a time as any to talk to her. "Mom, I'm thinking about staying here after the house is finished."

Faye laughed. "Why would you do that? This place is a dump! Don't worry! The house will be good as new when they finish."

"It's not that. I think I should have my own place. I'm thirty years old. I should be out on my own. And you're back with Caison again. You probably won't live in the house long anyway. I don't mind it here. It's close to work."

After cutting every piece of her pancake into tiny, tiny bites, Faye looked up at her. "You want to do this to hurt me, don't you? Because you don't want me to be with Caison."

"Mom, it doesn't have anything to do with that."

"No? It's funny how you linked the two as if to say, if you

don't see Caison, I'll move back home with you. Is that it, Sharyn? You don't want Caison to be in your father's place?"

"I'm not saying that. Not that Caison would ever take my father's place." Sharyn put down her fork. "I was saying that we both have our own lives now. I think I should be out on my own. I'm probably the only thirty-year-old sheriff who still lives at home with her mother! If I ever go to a sheriff's convention, they'll make fun of me."

Faye put her fork down defiantly. "Do what you need to do. I'm not willing to give up my relationship with Caison. It seems he's all I have since you and Kristie are too busy for me. But don't expect me to bail you out when it doesn't work for you! Living on your own is a big responsibility. I've cushioned it for you these past few years since your father died. I can't go on doing that if you live by yourself."

"Mom, I think I can handle it. I make a good living. Deputies who make less live on their own."

"Then you won't have a problem, will you? I've probably only been a burden for you since your father died. He was the one you really loved. He was the one who really understood you. I've tried but nothing I do is ever right."

"Mom—"

"So where is the bachelor party tonight?" Faye was finished with the subject. "Not that I can believe you're going to be Ernie's best man instead of Annie's maid of honor!"

"Annie's daughter is her maid of honor. And Ernie asked me. But let's not talk about this. Let's talk about both of us living on our own."

"Do you have any idea how humiliating it will be for me to stand there while my daughter gives Ernie Watkins the ring for his new bride? Half the town is invited to the wedding! I already feel like a fool. Maybe I should plan now to have a migraine. Are you wearing a tuxedo like the other men?"

Sharyn looked at her. She was beginning to feel like a recalcitrant teenager. "The party is at the Stag Inn Doe. No, I'm not wearing a tux. And why would it be humiliating for you?"

Faye put her hand to her heart. "*That* place! Do you know

how many times your father closed that place down? Who picked that terrible place?"

"Actually, it was Nick. I didn't know what to do for a bachelor party so I let him take care of setting it up."

Faye wasn't amused. "It's a good thing you aren't seeing him outside of work anymore! I always thought he had better social skills!"

"Mom—"

"What self respecting man would take a woman there?"

"Mother—"

"I hope Jack has a better influence over you!"

Sharyn shot to her feet. "I have to go. Thanks for the pancakes, Mom."

Faye bit her lip and called out for her daughter to come back. But it was too late.

Sharyn ended up at Joe's house. He was watching a football game on TV. He glanced at her when she sat down on his sofa. "Hey! What's up?"

"Nothing. How are you?"

"I'm fine." He looked at her again. "What's up?"

"Nothing. I wanted to see how you were."

He chugged some juice. "I only have three shots left. It's not too bad. I've been a little sick. But I don't think I ever looked as bad as you do right now."

She sipped some of the Pepsi his wife, Sarah, gave her on the way in. "I'm sorry. I couldn't go to Ernie's house. He's getting married."

"I heard that awful rumor."

"And Nick." She thought about it. "He's setting everything up for the bachelor party. I didn't want to bother him."

Joe nodded. "You're in love with another man?"

"No!"

He tapped his chin thoughtfully. "Wait. Don't tell me. We're on a roll here. I have no idea what you're talking about and you don't want to tell me."

"I should go." She got up to leave. "I'm glad you're better."

"Sharyn—"

Sarah heard him call and thought he was calling for her. She looked around the empty living room. "Where did she go?"

"I don't know." He picked up the phone. "But something's wrong. She's more skittish than a den full of rabbits!"

Ernie finally tracked her down in the Diamond Springs Presbyterian Church cemetery. She was wrapped in an orange plaid blanket and leaning against the back of her father's tombstone. "Hey."

She looked up. "Hey."

He sat on the frozen ground beside her. "What are you doing out here?"

"Sitting. What are you doing out here? Shouldn't you be trying on a tuxedo or something?"

"I did that. Joe called me. Right after your mama called."

"Oh."

He looked around. "I haven't been out here in a while, sorry to say. Never enough time."

"I know."

"Looks like there might be some ice crystals in that drizzle. Could be some frozen roads tonight."

"Yeah."

"When you were a little girl, I used to tickle you when you got moody. Don't make me do it again."

She looked at him and smiled. "I'm not a little girl anymore. I think it might be harder to do."

He waggled his eyebrows. "Want to give it a try?"

"Ernie." She laughed. "What would I do without you?"

"I don't rightly know. Same thing I'd do without you, I imagine."

Sharyn looked up at the ice crystals in the rain then looked at him. "I tried to talk to Mom about moving out this morning. She doesn't want to hear it."

He nodded. "And?"

"And she's thrilled that Jack and I are together!"

"You aren't together. You're with Nick. What's the problem? You have to tell her what you need to tell her."

"I don't know."

He drew a pattern on the hard ground with a stick. "I know Faye can be a handful. But she's your mama. You're gonna have to deal with her. Put your foot down. Tell her what you're gonna do and stick to it. Don't let her make you feel guilty. You're a grown woman. You need your own space."

"You never moved out on your own."

"I know." He sighed. "That was different. My mama was older and needed my help at home. I would've felt bad leaving her on her own."

Sharyn sighed. "I guess I feel the same. I feel like I should be there for her since Dad is gone. I know she's not sick or crippled like your mother was. And I know it probably won't be that long before she and Caison decide to get married again. I suppose I could wait. But I thought this might be a good time to let go."

"Might be," he agreed. "You and Faye have always been like oil and water. I know she loves her and you love her. When you're not together under one roof, you might appreciate that fact a little more."

"If she doesn't hate me for leaving her."

Ernie got to his feet. "She's not ever going to hate you. Even if you're my best man at the wedding which I know must be causing her some problems!"

"Yeah. You could say that."

He held out his hand to her. "You're gonna catch your death out here. Think how that would look. Sheriff catches cold and dies after sitting in cemetery. Come on. I'll buy you some coffee. Things will work out. You'll see."

She gave him her hand and he helped her to her feet. "Ernie—"

"You can back out on the wedding if you need to. I'll understand."

Sharyn hugged him tight. "I wouldn't back out on you!"

"I know." He wrapped his arm around her shoulders as they

walked out of the cemetery. "I guess that's why I asked you. I knew you'd keep me straight on this."

"I better." She laughed as she wiped the tears from her eyes. "If not, Annie will kill me!"

"You might want to give Joe and Sarah a call," Ernie noted. "They were pretty worried about you this morning."

"Yeah. I didn't want to bother you, and Nick was busy. Selma is caught up with this thing with Sam. I thought I could go and hang out there for a while until I could go back home."

He nodded. "Joe's as close to an uncle as you'll have. He could've handled it."

"I know. I'll call him."

The Stag Inn Doe was a ramshackle wreck of a place that sat squatly on the outskirts of Diamond Springs. It had been there for as long as anyone could recall. Some people in Diamond Springs called it a landmark and had photos of it from the '20s.

Most called it an eyesore and wanted to close it down. It had been the focus of several political rallies. But it wasn't quite in town so no ordinances applied to it. It was on the line between two counties so jurisdiction was obscure on it. It was the boys' spot to go on graduation night before heading down to Myrtle Beach. Most husbands only admitted to going there after their wives were out of earshot.

The present owner was Duke Beatty. He was a former stock car driver out at the speedway. His 30-year driving legend added spice to the club's reputation. Now no one could touch it because it was owned by a local boy who made good. He also owned the Cadillac superstore and three golf courses in the area. Not to mention half of an important NFL franchise. No one wanted to offend Duke Beatty.

"I have dreamed of coming into this place," JP said as he got out of his car outside the club.

"Bet your wife wasn't in those dreams!" David nudged him.

"I haven't been here since I came back from 'Nam," Ernie said. "My friends threw me a welcome home party here."

"It's kind of the same thing," Nick said, holding the door of his SUV for Sharyn to get out. "Think of it as the start of a new life!"

Sharyn looked at the place and wanted to get back inside the truck. She'd been out here on calls before. Usually drunk and disorderly arrests. Sometimes fights. She didn't expect to ever go inside as a patron.

"We have a room to ourselves if that makes you feel any better," Nick whispered when he saw the look on her face.

"Yeah. I feel better already."

"Look at Ernie," he pointed out. "This is where he wanted to come!"

He was right. She could see the look on Ernie's face. The Stag Inn Doe was a dive but there was something magical about it to all the men in Diamond Springs. "Okay. Let's get this over with."

They were fortunate enough to get a small team of deputized citizens to work the phones that night. Anything beyond that would mean that their pagers would go off at the club and at the Regency Hotel where they were throwing the wedding shower for Annie. Cari and Marvella were there with Trudy, Sarah and Faye.

Sharyn wished that she was there too. But she promised Ernie, so she put on a smile and they all walked into the club.

"Welcome! Welcome!" Duke Beatty met them personally at the door. His raspy voice and black cowboy hat were unmistakable. "It's always good to have the fine deputies of Diamond Springs here with us!"

"Thanks, Duke!" David said shaking his hand heartily. "I love this place!"

"Of course you do, son!" Duke looked at Sharyn and his eyebrows lifted. "Well, Sheriff Howard! This is an unexpected pleasure!"

"Mr. Beatty." She shook his hand. "I'll go with the unexpected part."

He laughed. "Call me Duke! I have your room ready gentlemen. And Bubbles is here!"

Joe grinned and Ed whooped. He and David slapped each other on the back.

"Who would've thought you'd be so good at planning a bachelor party," Ed complimented Sharyn.

Nick grinned at her.

"Duke laughs just like he does on TV," David told them eagerly. "I'm gonna ask him to sign my arm."

The inside of the Stag Inn Doe was worse than the outside. At least rain had a chance to clean the walls and freshen the stench. The carpet underfoot was sticky and a color that varied somewhere between red and brown. Sharyn didn't want to think about what she was walking in. At least she didn't buy a new outfit to wear to the party.

Duke showed them to the back room that Nick reserved. The music was blaring out some country song that was indiscernible. Several hundred people were talking and a race was being shown on the huge TVs. The lighting was poor but that was probably a blessing. In one corner of the room was a huge cake with a dingy, tilted light where the candle should be.

"There's Miss Bubbles!" David laughed and patted Sharyn on the back. "I wish more of us got married so we could do this more often."

The music started and the bubbles began coming out of the cake. The air was thick with anticipation. At the moment that the cake began to open, all of their pagers went off.

"Someone's tripped the wire in the surveillance house," Ernie said looking at his pager.

"Let's move!" Ed said with his hand on David's shoulder.

"Now?" David whined.

Chapter Ten

The new subdivisions were at the opposite end of Diamond Springs from the Stag Inn Doe. Even with their sirens on, it was 20 minutes away. Sharyn decided that they would go in silently. It would be better not to get caught up in a gun battle with the suspects in the house if they could help it. She believed that surprise was her best chance in cracking this case and putting the offenders in jail. That meant an extra few minutes getting there.

"I haven't had a chance to tell you," Nick said as he drove to the house, "but you were right about the thumbprint. It belonged to the dead girl. We'll have to wait for the hair because Bobby didn't keep a sample."

Sharyn nodded. "If I'm right about the rest of the gang, that will give us access to Lynette's room. We should be able to get a hair sample there."

"Which also puts you in line for anything else you can find to help Sam?"

"I hope so. Since we already have the murder weapon, that leaves us with the off chance that they haven't disposed of their bloodstained clothes. If not, we don't have much to go on."

"Unless one of them wants to confess."

She grimaced. "How likely is that?"

The three cars sped through the cold January night like a strange parade. They used the back roads around the city to be able to maintain high speeds. Many of the roads were single lane with tiny bridges spanning creeks and rivers. Traffic was forcing the state to build bigger roads to accommodate the new people in Montgomery County. But many of the roads were still the same as they were drawn on maps from a hundred years before.

"There are only two ways into that subdivision," Sharyn told Ernie on the phone. "Let's make sure they can't get out either way."

"You got it, Sheriff."

"Marvella and Cari are on their way too."

"Great," he said. "Annie will be thrilled."

"I'm sorry, Ernie."

"Part of the job."

Sharyn closed her cell phone and concentrated on the narrow road as they flew past cell phone towers that mingled with eerie tree shapes and farm buildings. "I'll be glad when this wedding is over."

"More tension than a murder investigation?"

"A lot more." She reconsidered. "Well, not more than this thing with Sam."

"Did you meet with Jefferson Two Rivers?" Nick asked.

"Yeah." She explained about his strange behavior. "I think he's worn out with worrying about what's going to happen. His brain isn't working anymore."

"I'm not superstitious," Nick replied, negotiating a turn. "But there are some things that can't be explained."

"Like a knife that makes otherwise good men kill women?"

"I don't know. I'm just saying you shouldn't dismiss evil out of hand."

Sharyn checked her grandfather's service revolver and put it back in her shoulder holster. She pinned her badge on her jacket. "I don't dismiss it. But so far the only evil I've seen hasn't been supernatural. It's been people."

As they turned to go into the subdivision where John Schmidt's house was set up for surveillance, a banged-up white Chevy van shot by them headed towards Rock Springs up the old highway that linked the two towns together.

"That's it!" Sharyn exclaimed as she got out her phone.

Nick swung the SUV around and followed the van.

"We're pursuing on Highway 16, Ernie. I think this is our gang. Call JP and David. I'm going to have Cari and Marvella stay with the house."

"Okay. We're right behind you!"

Sharyn told Marvella and Cari to check out the house carefully from the outside then stay there. "Don't go inside. Don't do anything or touch anything. Just wait in the car and make sure no one else goes in there. I don't want to take a chance on losing that videotape."

"Yes, ma'am!" Cari acknowledged.

"I don't think they suspect anything," Nick said, his eyes on the van about three car lengths in front of them. "They're running back as fast as they can but I don't see any sign of panic. They don't know who we are."

"I'm going to call the chief in Rock Springs. He could have something set up there for them."

"Good idea."

Sharyn waited for the chief to answer. "Let Ernie pass you, Nick. Let's not give the gang a heads up for as long as we can."

He nodded. "I'll call him."

"Howell Murray," the chief finally answered.

"This is Sharyn Howard. Sorry to bother you, Chief Murray, but we're in hot pursuit of an '82 Chevy van, white, license plate RTS 352. It's headed towards you. We believe it's the gang that's been robbing houses in Diamond Springs."

"You think they'll come in down Main Street?"

"I do unless they veer off from this course. Chief, I think this gang is made up of women from Piper College. Lynette Ashe was one of them."

"What? A group of college girls with plenty of money robbing houses in Diamond Springs? That's ridiculous, Sheriff!"

"Humor me, Chief. You can always report me again if I'm wrong."

There was no answer. Sharyn closed her cell phone.

"He reported you for snooping around?" Nick let Ernie pass him and dropped back a few car lengths behind him.

"Yes. But only to the DA's office. This time it could be to the state. I knew I was taking that chance before I got involved."

"Can't you report him for being an idiot?"

She laughed. "I don't think so. But if he fails to respond to my call, I can report that. We're *supposed* to work together."

"Yeah. I know how that goes!"

Ernie called. "They've ducked down a side road. No way we can follow without giving ourselves away."

She checked her GPS. "There's no road going in or an intersection that could get them out. Don't panic. Slow down and give them a minute, then go in. I don't want to scare them and have some kind of stand-off."

"Yes, ma'am!"

Sharyn and Nick, JP and David waited at the highway to hear from Ernie. When he caught up with the van, they'd move in.

He called a few minutes later. "I lost them."

"How's that possible?" Sharyn asked. "There's nowhere for them to go."

"I don't know. It's like they pulled off the highway and disappeared."

"Let's follow him in," Sharyn advised Nick. "Take it slow. They must be in the woods."

It was a rough dirt road barely wide enough for the cars to pass. Tree branches scraped sides and slapped at mirrors and windows. Without lights from the street, the darkness closed in around them, obscuring everything but what the headlights showed. There was no sign of the van.

"They disappeared!" Ernie got out of his truck when they reached him. He slammed his door closed. "Like they weren't even there!"

Ed followed him. "He's right! We waited a few minutes at the highway before we came in. Now there's no sign of them."

Sharyn looked around the dark woods. According to the GPS, they were sitting in 1,200 acres of state-protected forestland that went up to the boundaries of the school. There didn't seem to be any spaces big enough to drive a van through. The crude track ended only 100 yards or so into the woods. They all got out flashlights and stomped around on the frosty ground but there was no sign of the van anywhere.

"Look here," Ernie directed her. "You can see the tire tracks. They keep going. Right through the trees."

Sharyn shone her flashlight down on the dark red mud. He was right. There were tracks going everywhere, in all directions. All of them led up to a tree then continued on the other side like the van passed *through* the solid trees. "We need better light. They have to be here somewhere."

"We could go and get those spotlights from the office and set them up," David offered.

"Do that," she agreed. "We'll wait here for you."

Ed was crouched down beside the tire tracks. "This beats all I ever saw! My grampa used to tell stories about a ghost team of horses they followed into the woods once. The tracks disappeared."

An owl hooted from a nearby tree and a faint breeze rustled the fragments of dead leaves left in the branches. It was too quiet, even that close to the highway. Sharyn felt a shiver slide down her spine even though she knew there had to be a rational explanation for what was happening. Knives weren't evil by themselves and tire tracks didn't disappear into otherworldly places.

"I don't think these are ghosts. Look at this," Nick said, getting their attention.

Sharyn shone her flashlight beam beside his. Bits of net-like substance were hanging from the trees like moss. "What is it?"

"I think it's some kind of camouflage netting. They use it

in the military. It reflects light back creating an illusion while they get away from the area."

She nodded and crouched down. "So they drove into it and it fell back on them. But where did they go?"

Her cell phone rang. It was Chief Murray. "Where are you, Sheriff? I thought you'd be here by now?"

She explained the situation to him and gave him their location to the college.

He laughed. "Chasing ghosts, Sheriff? I'm going home if that's all you got!"

Sharyn ground her teeth. "Any *helpful* ideas, Chief?"

"Yeah. Check out Never-Never Land!"

"Thanks." She closed her cell phone. "Where did it go? The van has to be here somewhere."

Ernie shrugged. "I don't know. I can't figure it out."

"They must've had this set up in case anyone followed them." Ed glanced through the trees.

Sharyn sighed heavily.

"The van is probably still here, just camouflaged," Nick observed.

"Yeah in Vietnam we did things like that," Ernie agreed. "Once we get some light out here, we should be able to spot where it's hidden."

"You think they're still in it sitting out here somewhere?" Sharyn asked.

"Maybe." Ernie shrugged.

"It's the only explanation," she replied. "I guess we'll wait right here for light. I'm going to call in some highway patrol to help us search. If we get a large enough group, we should be able to cover every inch of this area until we find it."

"One of us should go back and view those video tapes before we go any further," Ernie considered, rubbing his hands together for warmth. "Or we really could be chasing ghosts."

"Good point," she agreed. "We don't even know for sure that they robbed the house or what we got on tape. We could also get a search warrant. Otherwise, they could walk out of here."

"I'll do it," Ernie volunteered. "You've got Ed and Nick out here for now. I'll send Marvella on out too. Cari and I can go through the house and look at the tapes. I'll call you about the warrant if it looks like we're set for one."

"Thanks, Ernie."

"It's gonna be a long night," Ed said. "Wish I'd brought some coffee."

"Me too."

"There's nothing much we can do until the lights get here," Nick suggested. "We might as well stay in the SUV and be warm. No point in freezing out here."

"Amen to that!" Ed grinned. "Too bad about the party, huh? I haven't seen Bubbles since I was in college."

Nick laughed. "I think Sharyn's just as happy that she didn't see Bubbles!"

Sharyn sat down in the SUV and closed the door. "I'm not going to think about Bubbles. I think we should all be glad they didn't have a drug raid while we were there!"

"They wouldn't do that to old Duke!" Ed protested, sitting in the back. "He's got everyone right where he wants 'em!"

Chief Murray and Officer Kaiser finally joined them as David and JP were returning with the spotlights. Marvella had already been there for an hour, sleeping in her car. A few highway patrol officers were waiting in their cars after getting Sharyn's call for assistance. It was almost midnight when the spotlights were put into place and the portable generator was fired up. When JP flipped the switch, brilliant light flooded the woods, illuminating everything. A fawn and a doe ran into the brush as everyone climbed out of their cars.

"Well, Sheriff, where's your ghost van?" the chief asked.

There was no sign of anything in the woods immediately around them. Sharyn looked at the ground. The tire tracks ran in every direction, all made by the same tires.

One of the highway patrol officers joined them. "What are we looking for here, Sheriff Howard?"

"We're looking for a van that disappeared into the woods about an hour ago. We were in pursuit and lost it right here."

The trooper looked around. "In the woods?"

She nodded. "I know it sounds crazy. But we found parts of a camouflage net that we believe they used to hide themselves. There has to be some kind of shed here or a place where they could drive the van and hide it."

The trooper nodded. "Okay. We'll check it out."

"Thanks." She shook his hand.

"As for the idea that any of the girls at Piper are responsible for any part of those burglaries down your way, I think you're getting desperate, Sharyn," Murray told her. "These girls are from professional families with plenty of money to see to their needs. They don't need to drive down to Diamond Springs and rob houses!"

Pike chuckled to himself at the idea.

"And I think we'd notice if any vans full of stolen property were rolling into and out of town."

Sharyn stared at them both. "Not if they had a way into the college from here."

The two men grumbled and muttered but they finally joined the search. Their conversation and coughing in the cold air punctuated the deep night. The scent of pine trees rose as they pushed their way through new growth. There were enough of them there that they could make a net and cover every inch of the illuminated property. Not enough to cover all 1,200 acres. It would take days.

Sharyn's phone rang. It was Ernie. "We got 'em!"

"Good. Are we sure it's the same girls?"

"I'm downloading several pictures right now to your laptop," he replied. "Let me know what you think."

Sharyn went back to the SUV and opened her laptop. She logged in and waited for the feed from Diamond Springs. Once she saw the images, there was no doubt in her mind that the burglars were the four girls from Piper College. "Good work, Ernie! Do you have a judge standing by?"

There was no response on the other end.

"Ernie?"

"Oh. Sorry, Sheriff. I was . . . what did you say?"

"Are you okay?" Sharyn asked.

"I'm fine. I was . . . I wasn't thinking. I don't know what I was doing."

She hunched over her phone. "Ernie, is something wrong? Are you and Cari okay?"

He cleared his throat. "We're fine, Sheriff. There was just . . . never mind. I have Toby Fisher standing by with Judge White. We're set on the warrants."

"Okay. I'm going to Piper to arrest those girls."

"All right. We'll be out with the warrants."

Sharyn looked at the phone, wondering what was wrong. She didn't have much time to think about it. If the girls weren't gone already, they were wasting time picking them up. She tramped back through the leaves and underbrush to where the others were searching. David was getting ready to move the lights.

"Sheriff, if there's something out here besides dead animal carcasses and leaves, I don't see it!" Marvella informed her.

"Let's keep looking," Sharyn answered as she walked past her. "Ed, give Doody Franklin a call. Maybe his dogs can find something we can't find."

"I'm on it!"

Chief Murray was half asleep against a modest sized pine tree. Sharyn woke him. "I'm going to Rock Springs to arrest these girls. Would you and Officer Kaiser like to come with me?"

He was startled. He glanced at her, then at the list of the four girls from Piper. "What's your proof?"

"We had the house set up. There was video footage this time. I viewed it from the car. It was definitely Lynette Ashe's four friends from her dorm. We also found Lynette's thumbprint at one of the houses. There's a strand of hair we think might be hers as well."

The chief was speechless but Kaiser wasn't. "You can't get a warrant on that!"

"I already have," she told them. "This was a courtesy. I'm going to Rock Springs to arrest these girls, with or without you."

She walked away and the two men scrambled after her.

Nick caught her arm as she walked towards the SUV. "I'll drive you there."

"They want to be there," she answered. "They just hate to admit it."

"I think you need someone to watch your back."

She glanced at him. "All right. There's not much anybody can do out here until daylight. All we can do is sit on the place and hope they make a move when they think we're gone."

Ed passed them coming from the SUV. "What's up?"

"We've got the girls from the college on tape. Did you get Doody?"

"He's on his way. He's gotta pick up one of his dogs from the kennel."

"Good. I'm leaving you in charge. I'm going to see if the girls are back at the college or if they've already packed up."

"Okay. Let me know what happens. Are you sure you don't need backup?"

Nick threw up his hands. "What am I?"

Ed laughed. "No offense, Nick. But you're a deputized citizen. That's not the same thing."

"It's fine," Sharyn told him. "The chief and Officer Kaiser are coming too."

"All the more reason," he muttered darkly.

"Thanks." She laughed. "But I need you here."

"Okay. I'm staying. Be careful. If you're right and these girls killed their friend, they won't hesitate to kill you."

"I know. I'll call when we know what's going on."

"I'll be glad when Joe gets back," he added.

"Me too!"

Nick and Sharyn followed Chief Murray and Kaiser back to Rock Springs. The tiny college campus was in darkness except for a few lights on the signs that directed people to the office.

"You aren't nervous about me being here, are you?" Nick asked suddenly. "Because we could go back and get Ed if you are."

"I would've left you there in charge if I was," she assured him. "I've wanted to drive this hog for a while anyway."

"Thinking about trading in your Jeep?"

"Not a chance! I've only got twenty-two more payments!"

Both vehicles pulled up outside the dorm at the far end of the campus. There were no lights on in any of the windows. Nick killed the engine then took out his .22 and checked it. "I'm ready."

"Stay alert. I don't want any shooting but I don't want you to get hurt either," she cautioned. "Their rooms are all up-stairs."

"You think they'll be expecting us?"

"I don't know. They're arrogant enough to think we don't know who they are without finding the van. They may not even be here. Right now, there are too many unanswered questions. The only thing we can count on is that they're probably armed."

He nodded. "I'm ready."

"Okay. Try to stay close, huh? I'd rather have you behind me than the chief."

"He'll have to push me down to get around me."

"All right. Let's go."

The dorm mother wasn't convinced that they should be in the house at all with their guns drawn. She flung herself across the doorway like she was trying to protect her charges. "I want to see a warrant!"

"The warrant is on its way," Sharyn told her calmly. "But the four girls we're looking for are possible flight risks and they may be wanted for more than the robberies in Diamond Springs. It would be best for you to step aside, ma'am."

The woman looked at the chief who nodded reluctantly and

pulled his gun. "I'm sorry, Marge. This is the way it's gotta be for right now."

"Haven't they been through enough with Lynette's murder and all? I can't believe this! It's an outrage!"

Sharyn stepped up and through the doorway, brushing by the woman in her pink flannel pajamas. "Excuse me. We're looking for Susan Atmore, Robbie Faggart, Bonnie Moss and Joanne Sikes."

"The two rooms across from Lynette's," the dorm mother spat at her.

Nick followed her immediately. The chief and his assistant consoled the woman a little but moved quickly not to be left behind.

"Those warrants better be here soon," Chief Murray warned Sharyn in a soft voice.

"We'll detain the girls for now," she promised. "If the warrants aren't here by then, we'll wait until they are to search."

He nodded and moved heavily up the stairs.

Sharyn kept her gun drawn and walked carefully up the old stairs. They creaked and groaned like an old man in his sleep. There was nothing she could do about it. If the girls were waiting for them, it could get bad. Her instinct told her that they were probably trapped in the van and not able to get back here. She could only hope her instincts were right.

There were two rooms across from Lynette's room. There were two girls in each room. Sharyn signed for the chief and Kaiser to take the second room while she and Nick woke the girls in the first one. She heard Nick inhale sharply when she knocked at the door. Probably hoping she'd kick it in, she thought, as the door opened slowly from the other side.

"Yes?" The girl in the white nightgown looked at Sharyn sleepily. Until she saw the gun in Sharyn's hand. "W-what's going on?"

"Robbie Faggart? You're under arrest for the robbery of a house in Diamond Springs this evening." She handed her spare set of handcuffs to Nick and moved into the room.

"W-what?" The girl faltered again in a pitiful voice.

Sharyn saw S-U-S-A-N spelled out in gold letters on the wall. Susan Atmore was bound to be trouble. She glanced at her empty bed and turned to face the bathroom just as Susan launched herself at her.

Moving fluidly, Sharyn watched the girl sail by her. She put away her gun as the girl came back up with a quick left hook. Sharyn ducked and kicked at Susan's feet. Susan fell hard on the floor but before Sharyn could pin her down, she jumped back up and threw a jewelry box at her.

Covered in wooden beads and jute, Sharyn ran after the girl and tackled her. She heard the air woof out of Susan's lungs and felt her go limp. Her head hit the creaky wood floor with a dull thud. Sharyn scrambled up to bring her hands behind her back and cuff them.

"I'm arresting you, Susan Atmore, for the robbery of 1425 Salton Place."

"I didn't do anything!"

"You have the right to remain silent. Anything you say can be used against you during your trial."

"You've got the wrong person," Susan screamed. "What are you doing here anyway? Someone call the police!"

"I *am* the police," Sharyn answered. "You have the right to an attorney. If you can't afford one, an attorney will be provided for you."

"Why are you doing this?"

"Do you understand these rights?"

Susan went mute. Sharyn hauled her up to her feet. Nick turned on the light and she noticed that both girls were wearing heavy white socks caked with red mud. "You should wear your shoes when you go outside. Do you understand your rights?"

"I understand that my parents are going to make you wish you never put on that badge!" Susan screamed.

Nick watched them. "Okay?"

Sharyn nodded. "Let's go."

By that time, the entire dorm was awake. It made Sharyn think again about the night of Lynette's attack. If everyone was used to her sneaking outside to smoke, no one would've paid much attention. Maybe wouldn't even notice when she didn't come back. But who was it that called the police to alert them? It was a man, Chief Murray said. With Marge the dragon at the door, she had a hard time believing it was a man in the dorm. On the other hand, Marge had to be letting them break the rules by going outside to smoke in the first place.

The chief had Bonnie Moss and Kaiser had Joanne Sikes. Both girls were crying. Both were still wearing clay-stained socks. "You better be right about this, Sheriff."

Ernie stepped inside the dorm as they were bringing the girls downstairs. The other ladies alternated between throwing their pillows at them and crying.

"This is ridiculous!" Marge said again. "You can't barge in here and take them!"

Sharyn gave her charge to Ernie. "I'm afraid I can, ma'am."

Chief Murray reviewed the warrants and nodded to Marge. "It's all up and legal."

"What's more," Sharyn continued, "you and I are going to have a conversation about how you're involved in all of this."

"Me? I-I didn't know."

"Really? I find that hard to believe after what I've seen tonight."

Marge patted the fat pink curlers in her hair. "I-I really don't know anything, Sheriff. I watch the girls but they sneak out sometimes. I do the best I can."

Sharyn opened the door to a sitting room. "Let's come in here, ma'am."

"Don't you say anything," Susan yelled to her fellow conspirators as they were led out the front door to Nick's SUV. "Don't you open your mouths! They don't have anything! Just shut up and stop crying!"

"Sheriff?" Officer Kaiser stopped her. "You've got the warrant. They're wanted in Diamond Springs but I think we should keep the girls here in our jail."

"I appreciate the offer, Pike. But you don't have the facilities. We'll take them to Diamond Springs. If you'd like to call their parents, that would be a big help."

Pike Kaiser nodded and moved away.

Sharyn sat down with Marge and they talked about the girls she arrested. All the girls were a handful, she explained. They all smoked and sometimes sneaked out at night to meet boys. If Marge caught them, she stopped them but she didn't always hear them. "What about the night Lynette was killed?'

Marge thought hard about it. "I don't really recall there being anything that night. A few girls were in and out after curfew. Not specifically Lynette. But she did smoke so she probably went outside and came back in."

"Could you be more specific?"

"No. I'm sorry, Sheriff." Marge smiled, lighting a cigarette. "Most of the time, this place is like a zoo! I'm lucky to keep up at all! They don't pay me enough, that's for sure!"

Sharyn saw the woman light up. She let the girls go out because she understood the craving but had to keep up the pretense of the dorm rules. "Have you ever known of any of these girls to go missing for a whole day or night?"

Marge thought about the question. "There was one night that I got an emergency call for Susan from her folks. I went up to her room and she wasn't there. Neither was Robbie. I checked with the other girls. None of them admitted that they were in their rooms. But I waited on those stairs for two hours thinking they'd gone out to smoke. I was ready to slap them when I saw them. Then I looked up and Robbie was going to the bathroom from her bedroom! I know I didn't fall asleep. I was so angry I couldn't. But there she was. I guess it was a big joke for them to hide her."

"Was Susan back then too?"

"Yes."

Sharyn closed her notebook. "Thanks. I'm sorry we had to disrupt everything."

"Did those girls really steal from houses in Diamond Springs?"

"Half a dozen times," Sharyn replied. "I appreciate your help. The DA's office could contact you to testify."

"All right. What will I tell their folks?"

"I don't know, ma'am. I appreciate your help. If you think of anything else, please give me a call. And I'd appreciate it if you keep those dorm rooms closed and locked like Lynette's for now."

"All right, Sheriff."

Cari was waiting at the door for Sharyn. She was staring out at the night that surrounded the dorm house.

Sharyn startled her when she put a hand on her shoulder. "Sorry. Are you ready to go?"

"Yes. Ernie went with Nick to take the girls to town."

"That's what I thought. Thanks for waiting for me."

Cari shrugged and followed her down the stairs. "Clean sweep, huh?"

"I think so. Good work on your part."

"We just looked at the tapes." Cari waited to see if Sharyn was going to drive. When she veered towards the passenger side, she ran for the driver's side.

"You and Ernie make a good team," Sharyn told her when she was behind the wheel.

Cari stared at her. "What do you mean, Sheriff? There's nothing going on between us!"

Sharyn laughed. "I meant working together."

Cari backed out into the road. "I'm not so sure."

"Why not?"

"I don't know. It's mixed up. Are we going back to town too?"

"No, we'll let Ernie handle processing those girls. David and JP should be on patrol. Drop me off where they're looking for the van."

"I-I don't have to go back and help process, do I?"

"What's wrong?" Sharyn asked.

"Nothing."

"Did you and Ernie have a fight?"

"No. Nothing happened."

Sharyn shrugged and let it go. She couldn't keep up with everything that went on in the office between her deputies. If Ernie and Cari had a little argument, they'd get over it. She showed Cari where to pull off the highway. She could hear the dogs howling and yelping before she got out of the car.

Ed met her when he saw the car pull in. "Nothing yet. The dogs are going around and around in circles."

"How could the van disappear so well that even the dogs can't find it?" she wondered, her breath frosty white in the night air.

"Beats me. Did you pick up the girls?"

"We got them. They were in bed, pretending to be asleep." She flexed her shoulder. "Well, except for one."

"But you're okay?"

"I'm fine. I was expecting trouble from her. She's definitely the leader."

Ed pondered the woods before them. "What about a metal detector? Maybe that would tell us something out here."

"Do it. I'll have the chief send some warm bodies to wait here so I can take Marvella and Cari home for the night. Let me know if you find anything."

Chapter Eleven

"The chief called," Ernie said as Sharyn stepped into the office. "He says he contacted the girls' parents but none of them are close enough to get back in less than a few days."

"None of them are juveniles either so we don't have to have their parents here to question them."

"Good point. Toby's here. He's in the bathroom. Nick is taking his kids out to the dorm to check it out."

"Ed is still working the site out there," Sharyn told him, unbuttoning her jacket. "The dogs weren't any good. He's trying a metal detector."

"Good thinking."

"What's up with you and Cari?"

Ernie's face blanched. "What do you mean?"

She shrugged as she grabbed a cup of coffee. "She sounded like you two had some problems."

"It's nothing."

"Okay." She looked at him. "Are the girls processed?"

"Yeah. The Atmore girl told them that they don't need lawyers because they don't have anything to say. I think we should start with one of the other girls."

"Works for me." She got a yellow legal pad while Ernie went down to bring Robbie Faggart up from her cell.

ADA Toby Fisher walked out of the bathroom and grabbed a cup of coffee. "I wish this kind of stuff happened during normal, daytime business hours."

She laughed. "Me too. There's not enough coffee in the world to make this look good."

Ernie went by with the girl in handcuffs. She was holding her head down but she'd stopped crying.

Toby sighed. "This seems like it should be easy."

"I'm glad you think so. Susan's had time to talk to them. It could be hard to get anything out of them."

"Well she doesn't want a lawyer. That's a good sign."

"We'll see." Sharyn grabbed a Coke from the fridge and took it with her into the interrogation room.

"Why am I here?" Robbie demanded when they were in the room with her.

"You're here because we think you and your friends, including Lynette Ashe, robbed seven houses in Diamond Springs in the past few months," Sharyn told her. "Coke?"

Robbie looked at the can. "How do I know you haven't drugged it or something?"

Sharyn popped the top and took a drink. "See? No drugs."

Robbie took the Coke and guzzled it thirstily.

"You girls have everything," Ernie began. "Why would you want to rob a bunch of houses?"

"We didn't steal anything. You don't have any proof that we took anything."

"We have you on video tape." Sharyn turned on her laptop and showed her the pictures. "They look like you and your friends."

"That isn't legal!" Robbie cried out. "You can't secretly videotape someone."

"This is legal," Ernie assured her. "We got a court order for it. That means anything we find on the tape is admissible in court."

Robbie glanced up at them. She combed her fingers through her thick red hair and smoothed it down on her shoulders. "That's not me. You can't prove it's me."

Sharyn sat down beside her. "What kind of proof do you think we need, Robbie?"

"Fingerprints. DNA stuff. Everybody knows that."

"We have Lynette's thumbprint from one of your jobs," Ernie said. "And we found some hair samples. Tomorrow, we'll have a court order to cut your hair so we can test it."

"Cut my hair?" she yelped in terror, clutching her hands to her head. "You can't!"

Ernie shrugged. Sharyn looked away and sipped her coffee.

Robbie grabbed one of Toby's hands. "They can't, can they? I mean the law wouldn't let them do that."

Toby blushed and looked away. "They can but—"

"If you work with us, that might not be necessary," Sharyn intervened before Toby told her how *much* of her hair they could cut. "You help us and we'll help you."

"What do you want?"

"I want to know where the van is. I want to know why you robbed the houses and what you did with the things you took."

Robbie sat back in her chair. "I won't tell." Her lips quivered but she didn't say another word.

"That's too bad."

"Of course." Ernie rubbed his chin. "They shave your head when they put you in prison."

"Prison?"

"What did you think would happen when you got caught? What did Susan tell you?" Sharyn wondered, looking at the young woman's tear-streaked face. "You've taken thousands of dollars worth of merchandise and cash. This isn't shoplifting some make-up from the store."

Robbie bit her lip. "You're trying to scare me."

"As a matter of fact, we are," Sharyn agreed. "Because one of you is going to tell us what we need to know. It might not be you. It might be Joanne or Bonnie. It could even be Susan when she realizes that we have her on tape. Whoever it is will get the deal from us. She'll be the one who'll testify and if she doesn't have a record, she may not go to prison at all."

Toby was listening so intently that he missed his cue. "Uh, yeah. Turning state's witness would be the way to go. I'll back the deal the sheriff makes with whoever tells her what she needs to know."

"Your parents will be here in a couple of days," Sharyn added. "You'll have to explain to them why it wasn't *you* who made that deal."

Robbie sobbed but didn't speak.

"We don't want this to be any harder on you," Ernie coaxed. "But we have to know what happened and how it happened."

"What if no one tells you, like Susan said? What if you never find the van?"

Sharyn smiled. "You sound like a smart girl, Robbie. You know about DNA and everything. You must watch forensics shows on TV."

"Yeah."

"Then you know we'll find out with or without you. We have a forensics expert from New York who can find anything. He's at your dorm room right now. If he finds what we need before any of you admit to what you've done—" Sharyn's phone rang. "Excuse me."

Robbie watched her walk out of the room with apprehension in her eyes.

"No sign of anything here," Nick told Sharyn. "It's just preliminary. It'll take hours to go through all of this junk. Why do young women have so many stuffed animals anyway? But there's definitely no size 12 Nikes. There are a lot of dirty socks. They have a lot of electronic gadgets, computers and such. We might be able to match them to what was stolen. No sign of any silver dollars either. But maybe they're in the stuffed animals."

Sharyn sighed with frustration but didn't let it show on her face. She knew Robbie could see her from the open doorway. "Thanks, Nick."

"Anything on your end yet?"

"I'll let you know."

She closed her cell phone and put on her poker face. She needed this girl to tell the truth. "This is your last chance, Robbie. We've found some preliminary forensic evidence that links these robberies to you and your friends. It will take a while to process it but when it's finished—"

"Okay!" Robbie yelled. "Okay! I get it! What do you want me to say?"

Toby dropped his notebook at her outburst. "You, uh, do understand your rights, don't you?"

"I know. I get a phone call, a lawyer, and I don't have to talk. Anything else?"

"That's it."

Robbie glanced towards the open door. "Just keep me away from Susan. It was all her idea. She'll hurt any of us who talk."

"What all was her idea?"

There was a scream from the basement. Ernie left them in the conference room to check out what happened. He ran back upstairs and grabbed the phone. "We need an ambulance. One of the girls is hurt."

"What happened?"

"The other two say she fell and hit her head. She's out cold and she's bleeding."

Sharyn went downstairs and found Susan Atmore sitting contentedly in the cell. The catlike smile on her face told the story. The uninjured girl was huddled in a corner with her eyes closed. The injured girl, Joanne, was lying on the cold tile floor. There was a large, darkening bruise on her forehead.

Quickly, Sharyn took Susan out of the cell she shared with Joanne and put her in a cell by herself. "You know, you may think this is the way to handle what's happened but you're only making it worse. And we'll have enough evidence to convict you of the burglaries. And Lynette's death."

Susan's eyes widened. She pursed her lips but didn't say a word. Sharyn knew she'd hit a nerve. The girl wasn't expecting anyone to link her to Lynette's attack.

The paramedics were there in a few minutes. They took the injured girl out on a stretcher while Robbie watched in awed silence. Sharyn knew they'd lost the battle even before she sat back down with her.

"I changed my mind," Robbie said. "I don't have anything to say."

"We can protect you from Susan," Sharyn promised her. "If we'd known she'd hurt any of you, we would've kept her apart. But you're friends. How can you stand her hurting Joanne like that?"

"Yeah. Friends." Robbie sat back and looked at the ceiling.

Sharyn had one last card to play. "She's always going to be there, Robbie. If you go to prison with her, you'll be seeing a lot of her. If you help us, we can keep that from happening. Susan has a record already. Did you know that? The rest of you are clean. If you decide to speak out, I could still help you."

"Thanks for the Coke. I'd like to go back to my cell please."

There was nothing more to say. Ernie escorted her downstairs. Toby sighed and put his chin on his hands. "That didn't go well."

"She's afraid. Susan reminded her what could happen to her. She was up here too long." Sharyn shook her head. "We'll have to hope we can get enough without them talking. But if we can't find the van or the things they've taken, we don't have much to go on."

"You have the video tape," he reminded her.

"Yeah. But a good lawyer will be able to talk them out of that. Without the stolen goods, we have four girls who broke into the house for a party. Not legal but not especially bad."

Toby jerked himself awake and got to his feet. "You've got your hands full, Sheriff. I wish I could help. But if you don't need me anymore, I'm going home. I'll see you later."

"Yeah. Thanks."

Ernie sank down beside her in one of the hard, ladder-backed chairs. "That didn't go right."

"You couldn't know. We've been assuming Susan turned on Lynette because she got greedy but she controls the whole group by brute force."

"She's a real fine tribute to her mama and daddy."

Sharyn glanced at the big office clock on the wall. "It's late."

"Yeah." Ernie yawned. "Now what?"

"Now we hope Nick can find something or Ed can find the van. And in the meantime, we come up with a plan in case they don't."

"I'm ready for a plan," Ernie agreed with her. "I don't have one but I'm ready for one."

Sharyn smiled at him. "Let's get some coffee and see what we can find out about Piper College. There's something out there that's bothering me."

"You mean besides the students being murderers and thieves?"

"Yep. There's that van disappearing into the woods and there's the thing with the dorm. Ernie, I think those girls are going in and out without using the front door."

"What makes you think that?" He roused himself enough to walk over to a computer and type in Piper College.

Sharyn explained her feelings from the first day when the chief told her that Sam dragged Lynette out without anyone hearing or seeing anything. "Marge told me about looking for Susan and finding her gone. Marge swears that she didn't come up the stairs and it made me think about it again."

"Who's Marge?" Ernie yawned. "And what are we looking for?"

"Marge is the dorm mother and we're looking for something about the college. Maybe before it was a college. I've heard the whole story about Elwood Piper using his home to create a women's college after the war. Since it was a plantation and most of the buildings were originally part of the plantation, what if there are alternate ways to get around on the campus?"

"My brain isn't working. It's either too early or too late, I don't know which. What kind of alternate ways to get around?"

"Tunnels? I don't know. But I think I remember reading about plantations that had tunnels that went from building to building. It was to keep food dry when it was prepared and it was raining outside." Sharyn snapped her fingers. "Thomas Jefferson! When my dad and I went to visit Monticello, there was something about tunnels that connected the house to the slaves' quarters and other buildings."

"So you think there could still be tunnels between the buildings at Piper?"

"Maybe. Let's see what we can find."

Ernie brought up historical records about Elwood Piper, including his picture. "Mean looking man."

"But obviously smarter than his contemporaries since he started a school for women."

"Still looks mean." He clicked on several entries under the Piper name. "That's strange."

"What?"

"I've heard people talk about how Piper created his school and so forth but everybody always assumed his child lost during the war was a boy." He tapped a key and a young woman's face came up on the screen. "Mary Randolph Piper."

Sharyn read the information. "She died in 1864. Doesn't say what from."

"People died from all kinds of diseases back then. I guess everyone around here thought it was the war."

"Which explains why he created a school for young women. Probably in her memory."

"I suppose it might. Here's a layout of the house from the history museum in Raleigh. There's a lot written about it because it was the first women's school of higher learning in North Carolina. Says here Piper managed the school himself from 1865 to 1895 when he died."

"He never remarried," Sharyn said. "That must have been odd in those days too."

"Didn't need a wife, I guess," Ernie quipped. "He had plenty of young women to take care of him."

"I suppose."

Ernie clicked on another line with the mouse. "This is weird."

Sharyn followed his reading. "I guess if the school has tunnels it wasn't famous for them."

"No but it was infamous for this other." He clicked on another line. "Look at that!"

A female student was found murdered brutally on the grounds of Piper School of Higher Education for Women. Her name was Elouise Hubbard. She was nineteen years of age on her last birthday. She was found stabbed to death near the library at the school. Her parents, Mr. and Mrs. Jonathan Hubbard of Philadelphia will come to see their daughter's body to its final resting place in the family cemetery.

"That's creepy." Ernie shivered.

"She was stabbed to death." Sharyn chewed at her lip. "Déjà vu, huh?"

"Yeah. That's *too* weird."

Sharyn's cell phone went off. "Sheriff Howard."

"We've collected a bunch of stuff from here," Nick told her. "I'm taking it back to the lab. I'll tell the dorm mom to keep the rooms locked and look at it again tomorrow. What are you doing?"

"Ernie and I are chasing ghosts."

"Any luck in the forest?"

"Not that I've heard. Go home. I'll talk to you tomorrow."

"Gladly. Let me know if you need me to do anything."

"I will. Thanks, Nick."

"Nothing, huh?" Ernie asked when she closed the phone. "Zip."

"That's what I thought. But look what I found."

Sharyn looked at the old newspaper report. "Two more? There were two more murders out there?"

He nodded, the monitor screen reflected in his glasses. "Yep. There's the first one in 1865. Another one in 1870. And another one in 1875."

"Coincidence?" Sharyn muttered, reading the rest of the report.

"All of them were stabbed to death, Sharyn. All of them

were women. All of them were close to the same age. None of them were local."

She shook her head. "Okay, my brain is fried now. That was over a hundred years ago. We aren't looking for the same person, Ernie. This has to be a coincidence. Or bad luck."

Ernie squinted up at her. "Or an evil knife that kills women?"

"That knife should've been in Cherokee back then, remember?"

He shrugged. "It migrated down here sometime."

JP and David came in from patrol. "Find that van yet?"

"Not yet. How's it going out there?" Sharyn asked them.

"Slow night," David answered. "It would've been a good night for that party!"

"Maybe we can do it another night," JP said with a broad grin.

"Ernie's getting married next weekend," David reminded him. "I don't think Annie would like him to be there on his wedding night!"

"I forgot," JP admitted with a slap to his forehead. "Next weekend is the blessed event."

Ernie didn't say a word.

Sharyn looked at him. "I'm going home."

"Okay. I'm staying for a while yet."

"You can do that tomorrow, Ernie. You won't be a bit of good to me staying here all night looking at this stuff."

"Are you telling me I *have* to go home?" he wondered, glancing at her.

She shrugged. "No. I guess not. I'll see you tomorrow."

"Good night, Sheriff."

" 'Night David, JP."

"Good night, Sheriff."

Sharyn looked back at Ernie as he sat hunched over the computer clicking on pages with the mouse. Something was wrong. She wasn't sure what it was but she was too tired to badger him tonight. Tomorrow, she'd have the truth.

* * *

Lawyers for all four of the girls were there in the morning. The girls didn't request them but their parents thought about it. By the time Sharyn came in, they had all spoken with their clients and understood the case. All of them agreed on a strategy. Keep your mouths shut.

Ernie was still there. Sharyn found him shaving in the locker room. He'd changed uniforms and taken a shower but the dark circles under his eyes told their own story.

"I hope you found something useful," she said, looking at him in the mirror.

"I don't know about useful but it's scary."

"More about those murders?"

"There was a girl murdered there every five years from 1865 to 1895. Sound familiar?"

She shrugged. "Not really.'

"The same years that Elwood Piper was president of the school. He died in 1895. No more murders."

"What are you saying, Ernie? That the ghost of Elwood Piper murdered Lynette with an evil knife that he got from Cherokee?"

"I don't know what I'm saying. But I've got another big coincidence for you."

"I think this might come from staying up all night."

"They were all murdered on January 19. Well, except for two of them. I couldn't find what day they were murdered but I have a call in to someone who should know."

"That was still over a hundred years ago."

"Was it?" He picked up a sheet of paper and handed it to her. "Look at this."

The print out was from two other murders. "Ann Johnson was killed January 19, 1965 and Becky Taylor was killed January 19 five years ago." Sharyn looked up at him. "Maybe I've had too much sleep. I don't see a connection. You can't possibly think whoever did those murders starting in 1865 is still alive and killing women."

"I don't know what I think. I don't know if I *am* thinking!"

He shut off his electric razor and stared at himself in the mirror. "Last night at the office, I kissed Cari Long."

Sharyn dropped the paper on the floor. "You *what*?"

"You heard me. Don't make me say it again."

"What happened?" She searched for words. "I mean, how did it happen?"

He sat down on one of the wooden benches. "I don't know. We were close, looking at the video tape. I looked at her. She looked at me. We kissed."

"Was it, uh, like a friendly kiss?"

He pulled the side of his collar down. There was a delicate purple bruise on his neck. "Not at all."

Sharyn sat down beside him. "Ernie, sometimes stupid things happen."

"Maybe it wasn't stupid. Maybe I'm not ready to be married to someone. Annie trusts me. But maybe I'm not worthy of that trust."

"What are you going to do?"

"I'm going to tell her. And I'm going to call off the wedding. What else can I do?"

"You could pretend it didn't happen. It wasn't like you had an affair with Cari! It was just a kiss. But it isn't worth giving up a lifetime of loving Annie. I think you should put it behind you. Marry Annie and be happy."

Ernie's eyes were dead in his face. "I can't."

Sharyn watched him walk to the door, not sure what else to say to him. Maybe he'd change his mind before he had a chance to tell Annie. Inspired suddenly, she said, "You're throwing away a chance for happiness that not many people get in a lifetime."

He looked at her strangely. "You sound like your daddy. Come on. Let's get to work. Do you know what day it is?"

She considered his question. "Sunday?"

"Sunday, January 19."

"Ernie, you can't really believe—"

"I'll let you know."

From the moment she walked out of the locker room,

Sharyn was deluged with phone calls from worried parents and demands from expensive lawyers. Not to mention the press.

Alan Michaelson, a former ADA in Diamond Springs, was representing one of the girls. He was wearing an expensive brown wool suit that matched his spiky brown hair. The gold in his tie set off the dollar signs in his eyes. He cornered Sharyn at the coffee machine. "Seems like old times, huh?"

"Except with you on the other side of the table," she agreed. "Oh wait. You were *always* on the other side of the table, weren't you?"

He ignored her remark. "You know you don't have enough to convict these girls."

"I have a video tape of all four of them breaking into John Schmidt's house last night. How much more do I need?"

"Come on, Sheriff. We both know if that's all you've got then these girls are going to get off with a slap on the wrist. What are you really after?"

She took him into the conference room. "We both know that if I get the smallest piece of evidence that corroborates these girls robbing seven houses that they're all going away to prison. What are the chances that piece of evidence isn't going to show up?"

"But you haven't found it yet. It might not exist."

"Which girl are you representing?"

"Bonnie Moss. And you're lucky about that because I won't be the one suing you for that girl getting hurt in her cell."

"Joanne Sikes was injured by Susan Atmore as a warning to the others girls not to talk. And I'll go a step more. These girls had a partner. Lynette Ashe. We *know* she was at two of the houses. We have hair and a fingerprint from her. I think we'll be able to prove that these girls, under Susan Atmore's control, attacked and killed Lynette Ashe."

Michaelson's eyes narrowed. "You'd have to have some good evidence to prove that theory. Especially since they're already holding a man for that crime who's linked to the girl."

"How much would it take? Nick has clothes from their

rooms. How much of Lynette's blood has to be on their clothes to prove that they killed her?"

"All right. What are you offering my client?"

"Protection from Susan Atmore?"

He smirked. "Get real."

"Bonnie doesn't have a record. I'm offering a clean slate on the robberies. I can't offer anything on the attack. That's up to the DA from Union County. But Lynette is dead. It was a brutal crime. I believe the other girls were afraid for their lives. I'd be willing to testify to that on her behalf."

"You'd get up on the witness stand for her?"

"Yes."

"Can I get that in writing?"

"Only after I have a confession from her on both events, a clear idea of everything that happened, and I know where that van is hidden."

He picked up his briefcase. "I'll talk to my client."

"By the way, what happened between you and Mr. Percy? I thought I'd see you back as ADA when he took Jack Winter's office?"

Michaelson smiled. "After being in the private sector, I realized there was a lot of money to be made. And Mr. Percy didn't want to completely shut down his private practice. He made me managing partner."

Sharyn nodded. "Congratulations."

"Thanks. I'll get back to you. I'll have to speak to Bonnie and her parents."

"Sure. Mr. Michaelson? Make it quick. If I get evidence before I get a confession, I'm charging them all. And Nick's been awake and working for a couple of hours already."

"I'll do the best I can."

Sharyn went to her office and called Nick. "Anything yet?"

"Quit pestering me!"

"I haven't even talked to you yet this morning!"

"Yeah? And that's how you start a conversation?"

"Did you get up on the wrong side of the bed or something?"

"I didn't sleep. I was up working on this all night."

Whatever Ernie had was contagious! She bit her nail. "You didn't kiss Megan or anything did you?"

"What?"

"Never mind."

"What made you ask an insane question like that?"

"Nothing. Never mind."

"Sharyn—"

"I have to get back to work."

"I'm on my way back out to the college. Come with me."

"I can't."

"There's nothing there right now that Ernie can't handle. Come with me. Please."

"Nick—"

"I'll come and sit in the parking lot until you come out. That can be for a few minutes or all day. Your choice." He hung up.

Sharyn looked at the phone then put down the receiver. She picked up her jacket and hat. "Trudy, I'm going out for a while. Call if you need me."

"What about the lawyers?" her office manager asked.

"Let them mill around. Michaelson might take me up on my offer but it will do him good to sweat for a while. Judge White is arraigning the girls this afternoon at two. I'll be back before then."

"What's up with Ernie?" Trudy asked in a lowered voice. "He almost bit my head off. And on Sunday morning!"

"Don't ask," Sharyn said. "Where's Cari?"

"She hasn't come in yet. Hasn't called either. Marvella is out with Ed. Ed said to tell you that he left someone going over the forest with a metal detector."

"Give Cari a call. Make sure she understands that this isn't her Sunday off. I expected her in here an hour ago." Sharyn wasn't going to let the office fall apart because something stupid happened between Ernie and Cari.

"Yes, ma'am."

"Thanks, Trudy. I'll be back."

"Good luck, Sheriff."

"Where are you headed off to?" Ernie asked when he saw her going towards the door.

"Back out to the college with Nick." She didn't tell him why.

"Cari's not here."

"I know. I'm surprised you haven't gone out and kicked her butt in here yet."

He looked away. "You know why I can't do that."

"Don't give me that," she told him briskly. "You handle personnel. Remember?"

"Yes, ma'am."

"Good. I'll be back. And Ernie? Don't work on that case from a hundred years ago, please. Let's stick with what's happening right now."

"Sheriff, you're being pig-headed about it! I'm telling you there's a correlation."

"Find me tunnels to look for the van. I don't want to look for a killer who's still alive after a hundred years."

"Yes, ma'am. But this other thing *could* come in handy."

"Thanks."

Nick was already in the parking lot behind the building. He was reading a forensics textbook and letting the engine run in the SUV. He looked up when she got into the truck.

"Nick, I—"

He leaned across the seat and kissed her. "If we can't start our conversations like that, can we at least say good morning or how are you?"

"I'm sorry."

He smiled and kissed her again. "Good morning, Sharyn."

"Good morning, Nick."

He put away the textbook and drove the SUV out of the lot. "I was up all night going through the clothes and toys we brought back with us. Nothing. I think we can assume that they change their clothes and take off their shoes before they come into the dorm. Wherever the van is, that's where the evidence is too."

"The dirty socks?"

"I think so. Red clay #1. Ordinary deposits. It could come from anywhere in this area. But there are so many of them that I think they must wear them after they take their shoes off. They're bulky too. Like you'd expect to find girls with ordinary size feet wearing to keep on size 12 Nikes."

"But not enough to convict anybody of anything but being stupid?"

"Exactly. But I had an idea during the night. Hair in their hairbrushes. It's possible we could find some blood in that. I've got Megan testing some washcloths we took but those are a long shot since we couldn't find any blood in their sinks. They probably washed up outside the dorm. These girls are smart. I don't have anything as far as the robbery is concerned. We went over the Schmidt house last night. They left it as clean as a rain shower."

Sharyn told him about her theory on the tunnels between buildings on campus. "It could even explain how the van disappeared. But the girls aren't talking."

"I take it the video tape isn't enough?"

"Not to convict them of all seven robberies. We need more than a single house break-in."

Nick turned the SUV into the college campus. The grounds were very still. A combination of cold weather and Sunday morning kept most of the students and faculty inside. He parked the car and shut off the engine. "Now, can we talk about why you think I'd kiss Megan?"

Chapter Twelve

Sharyn made it short, telling him about Ernie and Cari.

Nick shook his head as he grabbed his black bag and got out of the truck. "And you think that would make me and Megan—"

"You were both up all night." She shrugged. "Okay. It was a stupid theory."

He put his arm around her as they walked up to the dorm. "Yeah. But I like that you were worried about it."

"Thanks. That's not exactly the response I was looking for."

He stopped walking and looked at her steadily. "You never have to worry about that happening between me and Megan."

"I feel so much better!"

"Can we get on with this case?" he asked. "Or do we have to stand around and discuss our private lives, what there is of them, all day?"

Marge opened the door for them. She looked like she'd been up all night too. "Sheriff. Dr. Thomopolis."

"I need to pick up a few more things," Nick told her.

"And I'd like to take a look around, if that's okay." Sharyn followed.

"That's fine. I'm the only one here. The dean decided to move the rest of the girls out into other dorms until this is over. Do what you need to do."

"Thanks." Nick started upstairs.

"There's something I wanted to tell you, Sheriff," Marge

continued, stopping Sharyn. "I thought about what you said last night about the girls going in and out. Especially on that terrible night that Lynette got hurt."

"What is it?" Sharyn asked, taking a seat beside the woman on the old sofa.

"Well, I think all five girls went out together. They always do. They're very tight. Lynette was the newcomer to the group. She was a lot like Susan in personality. I thought there might be a conflict from the get-go. The thing is, what made me think that only Lynette went out, I didn't see the other girls come back in. But when they called about the attack, the other four girls were in their rooms. That's what made me tell the police that she went out alone."

Sharyn ignored the piece of evidence that the chief failed to tell her. Or did only Officer Kaiser know about it? "Marge, I think there might be another way in and out of the house. A secret door. I don't know. These old plantations used to have tunnels sometimes between buildings. Do you know anything about that?"

"No, Sheriff." She thought about it. "These are some strange buildings though. We talk about them all the time. Sometimes, they seem haunted. All the odd noises and strange goings-on."

"I'm going to look around. You know the house. Any ideas?"

"You know, there's an old laundry chute. We don't use it anymore. They say it used to go down into the basement when they kept the washing machines down there. It's been closed off for years."

"Where does it come up at?"

"The pantry. It's been boarded up as long as I've been here but I can show it to you."

They walked into the kitchen and Marge opened the pantry. "It's right there, under the potato bin."

Sharyn moved the wooden potato holder out of the way. There was red clay all over the floor under it. A place in the floor that had been boarded up opened easily now on new hinges. Under the board was a small square not quite 3-foot by 3-foot. She shone her flashlight down into the chute but couldn't see anything but more darkness. "Is there a way into the basement from outside the house?"

"Not anymore. It's been bricked up for years. They said it wasn't safe."

As much as it pained her, Sharyn knew she wasn't going to fit down that chute. She called Cari on her cell phone. "I need you out at the dorm."

"Sheriff, I can't make it in today. I'm sick."

"Cari, unless you're on your deathbed, I need you! How soon can you get here?"

There was a heavy sigh on the other end of the line. "Half an hour."

"I'll give you twenty minutes. Hurry!"

Marge looked at her. "Do you think those girls were crawling in and out of that hole?"

"Yes, ma'am. My deputy should be here soon and she'll go down so we'll know what's on the other end."

"I suppose it would be hard for you with your, er, big bones."

Sharyn nodded, refusing to let it bother her. "Excuse me, ma'am."

She walked outside to see if there was any indication of where a tunnel could come out. If the service tunnels were intertwined, only going between the buildings on campus, there might not be anything visible. Quickly, she called Aunt Selma and explained her problem.

"I'll meet you at Professor Neal's office," Selma said. "He's bound to know the history to the place. If there are tunnels, he'll know where they are."

Pike Kaiser caught up with her before she reached the Professor's office. "What are you doing out here *now*, Sheriff Howard?"

"My job," she replied. "And maybe yours too."

"You can't come in here and—"

"Why didn't you mention that Marge told you that Lynette

went outside to smoke at night? You knew no one dragged her outside. What was that all about?"

He squared his shoulders. "I was trying to save her reputation. I thought she'd been through enough. She could be kicked out for smoking. It's a strict policy.

"So you manufactured evidence?"

"What difference does it make? We know who killed her."

"Susan Atmore attacked Joanne Sikes in jail to keep the other girls from talking. Marge told me that Lynette was confrontational with Susan. The other three go along with her. They robbed those houses, Officer. And those four girls attacked and killed Lynette Ashe. Susan made sure they were all there so they'd keep their mouths shut."

"You can't prove it."

"No? Watch me!" She swung up to the professor's door. Pike stayed right behind her.

Aunt Selma was already there, holding her hands against the door so she could see in the tiny window. "I think he's here. I called his home. There was no answer. And I think I see his wheelchair right there in the hall. Good gracious! I hope nothing's happened to him!"

Sharyn shook the door but it was locked. "Professor Neal?"

Pike stopped her as she raised her foot to kick in the door. "This is my call, my turf, Sheriff." He pounded on the heavy door and yelled for the professor. There was no answer. He glanced at Sharyn then kicked open the door.

Selma started to rush in and Sharyn stopped her. If anyone was going to get hurt, she wanted it to be Kaiser. "Let the officer do his job."

Pike nodded then walked inside the office. He called back, "There's no blood. No evidence of foul play. His wheelchair is in here but I don't see him."

Selma followed him in. "Could he have fallen? Maybe he crawled away from the chair."

"I think the chair wouldn't be upright if he'd fallen from it," Sharyn remarked. She glanced around the office while

Pike and her aunt called for the professor and searched for him. She looked again at the cabinet where the knife was stolen. The brown leather book was still there. Carefully, she lifted it from the shards of glass and opened it.

It was the diary of Elwood Piper, dated 1864. In a sparse hand, he explained how his daughter Mary was stabbed to death in their garden by a Yankee soldier. *"The army caught him and prosecuted him. The captain shot him when he was found guilty. I cannot ask for swifter vengeance. They gave me the knife she was killed with, as though that token would ease my suffering. Instead, it has bewitched me. My thirst for vengeance grows apace with my hatred of those dogs who killed her. I do not know what I can do to appease this ache."*

The diary went on to reveal his efforts to 'appease his ache'. In 1865, he took the life of a young Yankee girl who was attending his self-proclaimed college for young women. For some reason, he waited five years and took another girl's life in 1870 with the same knife.

Sharyn skipped forward and found another entry from 1875 when he killed again. This time he wrote of hiding in the secret tunnels to avoid being caught after he left her body on the steps to the plantation house. A caretaker found her before Piper was gone. *"An angry mob from Rock Springs swarmed across the campus looking for the killer but never found me."*

Selma and Pike joined her again. Kaiser was on his cell phone.

Sharyn closed the diary. She'd have to borrow it from the professor. She knew Ernie would love to see it after his brief exploration into the past murders on the Piper campus. "Any luck?"

"We can't find him anywhere," Selma told her. "Something must've happened to him."

Pike got off the phone. "The chief is getting some men together to look for the professor."

"We'll help too," Sharyn told him. "There's already been too much death on this campus."

Pike nodded, for once not telling her to mind her own business.

Her phone rang. "Sheriff Howard."

"Where are you Sharyn?" Nick asked. "Cari's here. She's trying to stuff herself down an old laundry chute."

"Thanks, Nick. I'll be right there."

Selma stayed at the professor's office calling through his private list of names and numbers, hoping to find him. Pike went with Sharyn back to the dorm house. Cari was already in the chute. They could still see the light from her flashlight in the darkness as she descended.

"What do you think is down there, Sheriff?" Pike asked as they waited.

"I hope to find out what the girls did with the stolen merchandise and their van."

"Looks a mite small for a van."

The chief joined them about 20 minutes later as Cari was describing over the walkie-talkie what she saw in the basement. "It's a series of tunnels going out from here. They're about five feet high and about three feet wide. I can slouch down and get through to see where they go. It's really dark."

Sharyn considered it. "Be careful, Cari. We don't know which tunnels they used. Some of them might not be safe."

"You found them old tunnels?" Chief Murray asked.

"One of them anyway," Sharyn answered. "You knew about them?"

"Not exactly. I've heard tell that they existed. But people out here have seen the ghost of old Elwood Piper too. I didn't think the tunnels were real either."

The Silver Dollar Gang found out about them somehow. She thought about the journal in the professor's office. They took the knife to kill Lynette. They might have read the diary too. "We're hoping to find out where the girls put what they stole. Did you find the professor?"

"Nope. Not hide nor hair of him. Nobody's seen him since last night. His housekeeper says she left him at about eight with supper on the table. She said his bed wasn't slept in and he left his supper uneaten."

"Sounds bad," Pike considered. "Where could a man crippled up like that get to anyway?"

Chief Murray shrugged. "Beats me. Probably absent minded. I think he might've left to visit some relatives and not said anything to anyone. We'll be out looking and he'll be wondering why."

"Without his wheelchair?" Sharyn asked.

"You got a better theory?"

"No, not really. But that one doesn't make sense."

"Well that's why we're going out to look for him," Chief Murray said to her. "But it's most likely not going to amount to a whole hill of beans! Good luck with your laundry chute."

Cari called out, "I think I found something."

Sharyn started to call the chief and his assistant back then changed her mind. "What did you find?"

"It gets bigger. I can see light from somewhere, Sheriff. I—"

"Cari?" Sharyn said into the walkie-talkie.

There was no answer. Just a loud rustling sound.

"Nick, call Ernie," she said. "Tell him we need him here now! He's the only one I can think of who can fit down that chute!"

"Where are you going?" he asked as he picked up his cell phone.

"Outside. There has to be a way in from there."

"Sharyn!"

She ran outside to the spot where Lynette had been found. Crouching down, she examined the brickwork along that side of the foundation. Everything seemed to be in place. There were no apparent gaps in the bricks or mortar. But somehow those girls were getting in and out of the basement from the laundry chute. Or . . .

There was a small shed that was barely more than a few sticks left standing at the edge of the lawn before it met the woods. The wood was white with age, weather, and sun.

Maybe it had been a gardener's tool shed at some time in the past 50 years. Sharyn ran to it as Nick was coming out of the house behind her.

The door opened easily. The wind pushed it out of her hands. It squeaked but the hinges were new. And new wood supported the doorframe on the inside. Sharyn forced herself into the shed. At first glance there was nothing but some rusted tools and a few bald tires that were covered in dead honeysuckle from the summer. She kicked them aside and found what she was looking for. A trap door twice the size of the laundry chute entrance in the house.

"You're not going down there, are you?" Nick questioned as he helped her pull it open and tie it back. "Shouldn't you wait for backup?"

"Looks like you're it," she said, already putting her feet on the stairs that led down into the blackness.

"But I don't even have a gun," he protested.

She handed him hers. "Try not to shoot me."

The rotted wood stairs were slimy with clay and moss. The sides of the tunnel were thick with it. Once Sharyn got down to the bottom of the stairs, she found she could almost stand up. She walked with her head bent, shining her flashlight on the sides and floor of the tunnel. No more than 200 feet into the abyss, the tunnel diverged into three separate paths. None of them gave anything away, yawning like gaping mouths that could lead to terrible secrets.

"Which way do you like?" she asked Nick.

"I always go to the right," he answered softly.

"Let's go right then."

Sharyn started down the tunnel to the right. It was smaller than the first tunnel. They both had to hunch down and walk sideways to be able to get through it.

"The air is stale," Nick said. "Let's try not to suffocate down here, huh?"

"Sounds good to me. Look! I don't think you have to worry about it."

The narrow tunnel suddenly expanded into a wide cavern.

Huge boulders stood guard on the sides of it. Rotting wooden beams held the roof in place. Sharyn's flashlight beam picked up the side of a van. It was white and badly scratched by tree branches.

"License plate RTS352. Looks like we found the ghost van."

"Don't touch anything," Nick said. "This might be the answer to a lot of things, including your murder and those robberies. We have to preserve the evidence."

"So, why couldn't we find it from outside?" she mused, only half listening to him as she searched the walls in the cavern. "There has to be an entrance from the woods."

Nick was carefully opening the van door, letting the feeble interior light shine in the blackness.

Sharyn was walking up a gradual, flat incline. She could see the tire prints leading down and up from the cavern. When she reached its apex, she hit her head on something hard. Taking a step back, she pushed up against the roof with her hands. She was able to see a sliver of daylight from under the wooden door.

It was too heavy to raise by herself but she was willing to bet that it lay flat on the ground until they needed to get in or out. Covered by leaves and other debris, it would be almost invisible in the forest. It was wood so it couldn't be detected by a metal detector. Cleverly, the girls had covered the tire tracks by creating so many of the same that they couldn't tell which ones were real. They probably left it open when they went out in case something happened like last night. They ran through the camouflage net and into the cavern. The door shut behind them.

"Sheriff?" Ernie's voice crackled on the walkie-talkie in the stillness.

"Go ahead," she said.

"I'm down in the basement tunnel. I found Cari. Somebody hit her over the head but she'll be okay."

"Sure she didn't just walk into something in the dark?"

"From behind?"

"Okay."

"Where are you?"

"I found the van. Nick's checking it out. Call back for Megan and Keith when you get out with Cari, huh? I think he'll need them."

"How'd you get there?"

Sharyn told him about the entrance from the old tool shed. "There's a trapdoor in the forest. Wait 'til you see it. These girls were really clever."

"Not clever enough."

"Let me know when you get out."

Sharyn walked back to where Nick was examining the van under bright lights. There was a line of spotlights set up to run off the battery in the van. He had already located the five pairs of Nikes. Four of them were covered in blood. There were also bloody clothes.

"This is probably what you need for Lynette's murder," he told her. "And the back of the van is covered in silver dollars and jewelry. If we look around in here, we'll probably find the other stuff they haven't had a chance to fence yet."

Sharyn considered his find. "This should clear Sam. But Ernie says somebody hit Cari in the back of the head. All of the girls are in jail or dead. There must be someone else involved that we don't have yet."

"Maybe an adult mentor? This seems like a lot to do for a group of college girls."

"Maybe. I don't know about you but I had a lot of time to kill in college. I didn't think about doing anything this elaborate, but maybe I wasn't as smart as they are. Ernie's sending Megan and Keith down here when he gets outside with Cari."

"Is she okay?"

She nodded. "She's got a hard head."

There was a sound, like a whimper, from somewhere in the darkness.

"Did you hear that?"

Nick nodded and jumped down from the back of the van. "What was it?"

"Maybe the ghost of Elwood Piper. Today's his anniversary of sorts." Sharyn told him about the diary and what Ernie learned from the Internet. "The thing is that the chief was surprised that these tunnels were real. He's been out here for a long time. If *he* didn't know, who did? Besides the girls?"

Nick peered into the darkness. "Anyone who read the diary? You said Piper mentions the tunnels."

Sharyn thought about it. "You're right. And that could mean—"

The whimper came again. It was eerie in the total silence of the underground labyrinth. It might have been close to them but it could have been from the other side of the campus. Listening to it jarred Sharyn's teeth. She had to do something. "Let's go."

"Where?" Nick asked.

"Wherever that noise is coming from."

"Sharyn, we have one gun and a flashlight. If we run into trouble—"

The whimper came again. It was a feeble, muffled call for help.

"Then we'll have to hope we outnumber whoever it is." She started forward into the darkness with her flashlight shining like a pinpoint of light in the void. She hugged the wall, hearing Nick's breath behind her as he stayed close to her.

They came to another fork in the tunnels. Nick held her back. "Wait. If we hear the noise again, we'll know which way to go."

They stood and waited. Minutes ticked by on their silent watches. Above them, the world was sunshine and fresh air. Their world was reduced to an awareness of themselves and the heavy burden of earth above their heads, the smell of the ground and the dampness. Finally, the sound came again. It was high pitched, like a moan. Distinct and rending. A soul frightened beyond fear, a hopeless crying wail.

"This way," they both agreed, starting towards it.

"Have I told you how wonderful it's been these last few months?" Nick whispered, touching her arm. "I've loved being with you. And it doesn't have anything to do with you being the sheriff. In fact, at moments like this, I wish you *weren't* the sheriff."

Sharyn put her hand across his lips and stood still. There was another noise that didn't sound like fear. It was the inexorable tread of heavy boots coming from a long way off down the empty tunnel. She turned off the flashlight.

"I've had a good time, too, Nick," she said in a whisper near his ear. "But I don't plan on dying here. In fact, I'm inviting you to dinner next weekend after Ernie's wedding. Can you make it?"

"Dinner? Not just popcorn? I'll be there!" His breath brushed the side of her neck.

"Okay. Let's see what's up here!"

Sharyn pushed forward into the tunnel that led off to the left. It was smaller, shorter like the one that led to the cavern with the van. It was awkward holding her head at the angle she needed to get through and still keep an eye out for whatever was at the other end. It could open up at any moment and they would be exposed.

The heavy boots stopped walking. So did Nick and Sharyn. They pressed themselves against the side of the tunnel, barely daring to breathe. There was a candle flickering in the darkness about a hundred feet in front of them. Its feeble light wasn't enough to give away their position.

Sharyn saw what looked like a rusted wash pan turned over and used for the base of the candle. Beside it rested the knife that Jefferson Two Rivers had called evil.

Not far from there was a young woman bound hand and foot, lying on her side with her face in the clay. A dirty gag was stuffed in her mouth. She was wearing a pale green nightgown. Her golden brown hair spilled across her face. She tried to move it out of her line of vision but her efforts were wasted. She tried to look around to see what was going on but couldn't move enough to tell.

On the other side of the opening, barely visible in the light, was a man. He was crouched down, facing the light. His head nodded up and down and he was mumbling like he was conversing with someone they couldn't see. A black hood covered his head. His eyes gleamed through the slits cut for them.

The girl on the floor whimpered again. The man got up. His boots tread heavily across the hard clay towards her. "For Mary."

"That's enough of that weird stuff! Get down on the ground and put your hands behind your head!" Marvella's clear tenor voice sang out.

The man looked at her. Then he leaned forward and the breeze gutted the candle.

There was movement in the void. Nick pushed Sharyn to the ground as someone rushed past them. A gunshot rang out, echoing through the tunnels. Sparks illuminated the blackness so thick that it was like being blind. Marvella swore and ran into the wash pan, tripping over it.

Sharyn took a deep breath and clicked on her flashlight. Marvella was on the ground beside the young woman. Neither one of them appeared to be hurt. The man in the black mask was gone. So was the evil knife.

"Marvella?" Sharyn got to her feet.

"Sheriff?" She looked around. "I messed up. I tracked that sucker here. I think he was the one who hurt Cari. Who's this girl?"

Nick was kneeling beside the girl, helping her sit up and taking the gag out of her mouth. "Are you okay?"

"I-I don't know. I was sitting in my room and something came out of the wall at me. It was a man. He hit me and dragged me here. Where did he go?"

"Good question," Nick said. "Let's worry about getting out of here for right now. Can you walk?"

"I think so."

"You okay, Sheriff?" Marvella asked.

"I'm fine. How about you?"

"Except for feeling like a chump! I should've waited for back up. I should've been more careful."

Sharyn reached down to the floor beside her and touched the thick red spots. "I think you hit him."

"Really?"

"It might be the only way we'll know who he is," Sharyn said. "Good work, Deputy."

Marvella grinned. "Thanks, Sheriff. I did it, you know? Something important. Just like I told you."

Sharyn smiled and patted her shoulder. "You're right. Now let's find this guy before he gets to do this again. Nick, can you get her out of here?"

"Sure. Do I get the flashlight?"

"I have one too," Marvella volunteered. "Is there a medal for something like this?"

Sharyn nodded. "Look at that girl's face. She had to know she was dead. That'll stay with you longer than a medal."

"Yeah." Marvella sighed. "But *is* there a medal?"

Sharyn's cell phone rang as she and Marvella left the old tool shed. They'd managed to find their way back out of the maze of tunnels. The trail of blood they were following ended abruptly. The man must have realized he was leading them. They were forced to re-trace their footsteps to avoid getting lost. Nick and the girl were already clear. Red lights flashed from several paramedic vans and squad cars on the street.

"They found the professor," Selma told her. "That chair we found was his spare. He was thrown out of his, coming across the campus from the main office. He's hurt a little but he'll be fine."

"Really? That's great, Aunt Selma." Sharyn's mind was ticking away at the facts.

"Where are we looking first, Sheriff?" Marvella asked eagerly. "Let's get this guy!"

"I want you to find Chief Murray and bring him to the professor's office," Sharyn told her. "I'll meet you there."

Marvella's dark face fell unhappily. "But Sheriff—"

"Get there as fast as you can."

"Yes, ma'am."

"And leave your walkie-talkie on."

"Okay."

Sharyn walked slowly back to the professor's office. His door still hung back on its hinges where Officer Kaiser had kicked it in. She sat down behind his desk with the old diary. As she skimmed forward, she came to a date. January 19, 1965.

"Oh, Sharyn!" Selma said with a smile as she wheeled the professor into his office a few moments later. "Did you find what you were looking for?"

"And then some." She looked at Aaron Neal. "How are you doing, Professor Neal?"

"I'm much better now." He sniffed. "Probably catch my death of cold after lying out there on that cold ground. Would anyone like some tea?"

"I was looking at this diary." Sharyn thumbed the pages. "I hope you don't mind. My deputy's been doing a little research into the murders that happened here between 1865 and 1895. All of them were the same. A young northern girl murdered with a knife every five years. Her body found on January 19 somewhere on campus."

The professor's eyes narrowed.

"Like the last two murders," Sharyn continued, "the one in 1965 and the one five years ago. That made it time again, didn't it? Time to avenge Mary Piper's murder."

"Sharyn?" Selma demanded. "What are you saying?"

"She's right, Selma," the professor acknowledged. "Those murders happened here. Grisly stuff. They were committed with that knife that was stolen from me. All of them. It was the same knife that killed Mary Piper. The Cherokee legend says that it's evil. They have a word for it."

"*S-gi-na,*" Sharyn supplied.

"You've done your homework."

"The same knife that almost took a life tonight." Sharyn sat forward and put down the diary. "Because today is the nineteenth of January and it's been five years. Hasn't it?"

"Yes, it has. I find ritual so comforting, don't you, Sheriff?"

"You were going to kill that girl in the tunnel. My deputy shot you. Was it in the arm or the leg?"

"Sharyn!" Selma rounded on her. "The man can't walk!"

"I think a miracle happened, Aunt Selma. I think the professor can walk now. He's been able to for the past five years. Right, Professor?"

Aaron Neal smiled slowly. "Even if what you were saying were true, Sheriff, you have no proof. Can the girl identify me? Do you know where the knife is?"

"I have these two modern journal entries. And I have a feeling if we searched you for the bullet hole and the knife, we'd find both, sir. Everyone else around here thinks the tunnels are a myth. The girls believed it and took advantage of it because they read it in your journal. You knew they took your knife and called the police about Lynette. After all, it wasn't time for another girl to die yet, was it?"

With a speed that belied his crippled form, the professor shot to his feet and knocked Selma aside to the floor. Sharyn moved her head a fraction of a second before the knife would've struck flush in her right eye. It thudded into the wood panel behind her.

Chief Murray and Officer Kaiser were on him in the next instant. They pushed him to the floor and forced his hands behind his back. The professor groaned as blood spurted from the wound in his right shoulder.

Marvella moved in to help Selma to her feet. Sharyn took a deep breath and realized that for a moment, she had stopped breathing. She turned and looked at the markings on the handle of the knife. She'd come close to being another notch. Ernie and Nick followed everyone else into the office. She got to her feet, hoping that no one would notice her hands trembling.

Epilogue

Sharyn was sitting in the kitchen, reading the newspaper account of Sam's release. There was a picture of him hugging Aunt Selma outside the jail in Unionville. What the paper didn't tell was that the DA was lucky to get a confession from Professor Neal. The knife he used to murder the two women was missing.

Privately, Sharyn thought that Jefferson Two Rivers had some part in that but she wasn't interested in following it up. The evil knife was gone. Maybe there was something to its legend. Something had seduced a normal man into becoming a crazed killer.

All of the young women she arrested were being held without bail for Lynette's murder and the house robberies. After being forced to excavate the truth, Sharyn wasn't interested in cutting any deals with them. Mr. Percy was another story, but that was out of her hands.

The phone rang. Her mother was out for the night, so she answered it. "Hello?"

"How are you, Sharyn?"

It was Jack Winter. "I'm fine. My mother is out with Caison. You'll have to try back."

"Actually, I called to talk with you. If you're not busy tonight, maybe we could go out for a drink?"

Sharyn shuddered. "I don't think so. Thanks anyway."

"I understand." His voice was quiet, carefully modulated.

Creepy. "By the way, I love that new shade of pink you started using on your toenails."

Sharyn started to speak but the line went dead. She put the phone down carefully and closed all the blinds in the apartment.

Outside on the cold street, Jack Winter laughed and had his driver pull away from the curb.